PRAISE

"A wild philosophical ride that is as funny as it is timely and as mind expanding as it is mind bending."
Daria Sommers, award-winning director, writer and producer

"Zany and off-the-wall imaginative, *Bertram's Emporium of Things People Say* fires fast-paced jabs at the excesses of 21st century cancel culture, militant ideology, and alternative facts, with plenty of plain ol' fun thrown in for good measure."
Ian M. Rogers, author of *MFA Thesis Novel*

"Brilliant!"
Alycia Vreeland, author of *Baby Darlin'*

"We all need to see ourselves in the mirror, so we don't take ourselves too seriously. Get up to speed with this comment on our times—and for a good laugh."
Rusty Allen, author of *Ella's War*

"Poking fun at the modern world has never been so much fun. A satirical gem!"
The Wishing Shelf

ABOUT THE AUTHOR

From Colombia to Israel to Canada, and in the process, from Judaism to apostasy via philosophy, Ariel Peckel is of no fixed identity. He obtained a PhD from the University of Toronto in philosophy of religion with a focus on the Enlightenment and on modern naturalism and atheism, writing a dissertation on Hume, Nietzsche, and Wittgenstein. He has published an award-winning article in the journal *Hume Studies* (2024), and divides his time between academic writing and satirical social commentary, aspiring to refine the art of tipping sacred cows in both domains.

arielpeckel.com

BERTRAM'S EMPORIUM *of* Things PEOPLE SAY

ARIEL PECKEL

www.vineleavespress.com

Bertram's Emporium of Things People Say

Print Edition
ISBN: 978-3-98832-091-9
Published by Vine Leaves Press 2024

Cover design by Jessica Bell
Interior design by Amie McCracken

To the memory of my beloved aunt, Becca. Who always had a bottle of tequila in the trunk of her blue Volkswagen Beetle. Who was a kaleidoscope propelled by rocket fuel. Who, as she lay dying in hospice, hollowed-out and muted by aphasia, stuck out her tongue and smiled as if to say, "Even now, I refuse to go out with a whimper."

AUTHOR'S NOTE

This book does not take aim at persons but ideologies, on both sides of the spectrum—or horseshoe—that deny facts and forbid dissent while harming the very institutions, ideas, and people they pledge to defend.

On one end of the horseshoe, far-right calls for untrammeled freedom from government intrusion are conveniently reversed the moment religious education and reproductive rights are at issue, whereupon sweeping government control is suddenly sacrosanct. Cults of personality flourish in that ideological corner, with its figureheads gaining levels of adulation, infallibility, and unchecked authority that were, just last century, a more frequent sight among their sworn enemies on the radical left. But despite that ideological chasm—which is the precise distance between the two ends of a horseshoe—the primary beneficiaries of the ruin that such leadership leaves in its wake are the same in every case: persons, often the ones the leaders claim to serve.

Across the horseshoe, militant gender identity ideology erodes the rights of the persons it claims to serve. It denies universally accepted biological traits that protect women's right—along with biological sciences that make gender reassignment procedures possible for trans people—while advancing revisionist conceptions of women that erase them, as women, from their historical and present struggles. At gunpoint of that ideology, parents and physicians are pushed into overhasty and rash approval of procedures like hormone blocking and castration for gender non-conforming children, which can be life-renewing for trans people, but cause life-lasting harm to detransitioners.

In the vast midland of the horseshoe, countless persons believe, in private, that the time has come to knock those ideologies off their pedestals. This author believes it is time to publicly laugh them off.

YES, WE'RE OPEN

9:27 AM

Like the chicken and the egg before it, what you see around you was hatched by an idea. Can you smell it, the tangy afterbirth of innovation? Then come in closer. And shut that door behind you.

Rome may not have been built in seven days, but the world was. And like the cosmic wizard responsible for it, I have created this world as one would a certain whimsical chocolate factory of fame: on the backs of height-divergent people of color—burnt sienna, specifically.

"How did it all begin?"

I'm glad I asked. An old acquaintance once told me, "You're a connoisseur of the human condition, Bernice. What doohickeys and knickknacks are must-haves for the human specimen today?"

"I'll do you one better," I said. "I'll make a catalog. And it's Bertram. Bee-Ee-Ar-En-I-Cee-Ee."

BERTRAM'S CATALOG OF GIZMOS FOR THE MODERN HUMAN SPECIMEN

THE WRISTWATCH

We've all heard that time is an illusion. But have you heard that time is *not* an illusion? With the new Wristwatch, you don't have to. Just consult the clockface, read the minute and hour hands, and get your pocketbook ready because you're about to make reservations and keep appointments!

Sure, it may not have the devil-may-care bravado of living in the nontemporal moment. But such timeless titillations belong in the dustbin of history, alongside other outdated devices, like calendars to keep track of those pesky crop cycles, or time zones to coordinate the bourgeois tasks of communication, labor, travel, commerce, and government.

With The Wristwatch, illusions are a thing of the past. So don't be the one blazed boob saying, "Time must go." Be the trailblazing boss saying, "Time *to* go."

THE PEDOPHILE WHISTLE

They lurk in shadows, skulk in alleyways, and conceal themselves in covered playground slides. No, I'm not speaking of *Procyon lotor*, otherwise known as the raccoon. I am speaking of a more elusive predator, outfitted with the stealthiest traits that natural selection has to offer.

Its cunning is unrivaled in the animal kingdom, baiting its prey the way a catfish does guppies. Its furtive glance peeks through peepholes in newspapers while its victims are none the wizened. The pedophile knows no rival, no threat, no mortal enemy.

Until now.

Introducing The Pedophile Whistle. With its ergonomic design and range of up to 200 decibels, The Pedophile Whistle finally gives us the edge we need *over them.* All it takes is for a pedophile on the prowl to grasp The Pedophile Whistle, and then blow it. A single blow into The Pedophile Whistle by an average pedophile will create a sonic emission so disruptive, it is guaranteed to betray the user's location in mere seconds. It is particularly effective with pedophiles in close quarters.

"Turn around! I heard something behind us—a *whistle* of some sort."

"Not of some sort. Of the *pedophile* sort. There it is! Grab it before it gets away!"

Swish! Zabbadap! Plop! Pedophile subdued!

"Thank you, The Pedophile Whistle!"

The Pedophile Whistle. No more lesting.

(*The Pedophile Whistle is not for everyone, only pedophiles. It is not advised to use The Pedophile Whistle if you have a medical history of not fantasizing about the legally underaged. If you experience illicit erotic urges after not using The Pedophile Whistle, it is recommended that you speak with a professional who can prescribe The Pedophile Whistle to you.)

THE PRONOUN SIMULATOR

Navigating pronoun preferences can be a landmine/land-ours. Studies estimate that the majority of men and women conform to the pronouns "him" and "her," respectively. We call such people Dupes of the Patriarchy. But those days are over. With our official "As Seen on TikTok and in Gender Studies 101" seal of approval, The Pronoun Simulator allows *you* to perform your way out of the impositions of obstetric power structures in the drop of a tantrum!

"Hold the phone, you old so-and-so! I thought that stressing pronoun preferences was a way for trans people to be recognized by the pronoun that matches their reassigned gender."

Not anymore, it isn't! With the backing of experts in decolonized biology and sex neuroscience from world-renowned laboratories of quantum postmodernism, gender dysphoria is no longer a possession of the few, but is equitably democratized for *all* to claim victimhood to. With The Pronoun Simulator, no bodily discomfort is too trivial to self-diagnose as disaffected, no grievance too minor to disqualify *you* from swelling the ranks of the minority. Had a bad case of the monthlies? Then ditch that fallopian "she" pronoun and brandish a bold statement-making selection from our roster of over three hundred destabilizing designs, including such classics as "zer," "zhou," and "schwa." So what are schwa waiting for? Start lecturing others about the heteronormative problematicity of bio-essentializing modes of discourse today!

"I thought you were going by 'vlem,'" they'll say.

And you'll say, "I go by 'those/thars' now. Don't you know I had an ungendering case of flatus on Monday? And your assumptions about my identity based on decommissioned pronouns from last week are postcolonially microaggressive. I'm reporting your misconduct to HR."

Get someone fired—and yourself *fired up* for The Pronoun Simulator!

** Order The Pronoun Simulator today and we'll include a selection from J. K. Rowling's Harry Potter series for you to boycott, free of charge. **

THE LIE DETECTOR

Recent spikes in "facts" and "experts" have made it more difficult than ever to determine what is true. That's why we here at Bertram's came up with The Lie Detector. The Lie Detector uses a series of skeptical strategies to test the validity of the most enduring myths of mainstream "science." The following is a real-life debunking of an astrophysicist's "truths" using our state-of-the-art Lie Detecting methods.

"You say a man landed on the moon. *Which* moon, I ask? And moreover, which *the*? I see new moons in the sky every night, and they look completely different from each other; some are even shaped like bananas. In addition, I can barely jump two feet in the air. You expect me to believe that someone soared even higher and landed *precisely* on one of the daily moons? Sure, basketball players can jump higher than two feet. But I've never met one, so I can't discount the possibility that they aren't simulations. In fact, I can't rule out that *you* are not a simulation, and that in reality you're not just a half-eaten casserole in a '90s sitcom. Speaking of the '90s, how can I be certain of whether that era actually happened, since it is *only* in my memory? Therefore, it is not entirely unimpossible that it doesn't just not exist solely in my memory. What's more, I cannot ascertain beyond the shadow of a doubt that it is indeed my memory and not Genghis Kahn's. And what if it is not Genghis Kahn's memory, but an aspiring proctologist's mustache wax? I rest my case."

With these and such techniques, you too can do your own research and become a truth-sleuth—and *that* is no lie.

So purchase The Lie Detector today. Because there isn't nobody who can't disprove that infanticidal reptilians don't rule the unround Earth.

THE GUITAR

Australian men are known for being soft-spoken, aristocratic, and for not clustering into gaggles of wankers when they run into each other at hostels. Consequently, Australian men struggle with being heard and seen. Enter The Guitar. Contrary to what leather-clad headbangers surrounded by chicks might suggest, The Guitar looks cool on men—especially Australian men.

Think about it, ladies. You all know at least one Australian man: mild-mannered, urbane, willing to listen to others while keeping his penetrating thoughts on how time is an illusion to himself. Now strap

The Guitar on him and put him by a bonfire: *total transformation*. What was before a stickler for manners is now "sticking it to The Man," or as they say in Australia, "scrimshaggling The Mate."

Sit back and witness as the guitared Australian man overcomes his introverted nature and gives voice to his melancholy soul in a rendition of "Wonderwall" by Oasis. The flickering flames lick his bare chest, behind which lie the untold profundities of a heart that has been thirsting for so long to be noticed. And you think to yourself, "I could scrimshaggle that man tonight." But just as you believed that this night—this oceanic night, riddled with complexity of meaning—had reached its mystic apogee, just then, the Australian man summons his peers. Now, toward the dancing fire, auburn-tressed Australian men make their way, Guitars slung across their chiseled torsos. Torrents of passion, heavy as quicksilver but delicate as silk, begin cascading from them, as they fuse chords and souls in a rendition of "Iris" by Goo Goo Dolls. You feel your very essence slip through your fingertips and melt into the air. And you think to yourself, "I could scrimshaggle any one of those men tonight."

The Guitar. Scrimshaggle a sheila tonight, mate.

THE ABORTION AVATAR

Recent gender studies' deconstructions reveal that feminocentric narratives of human pregnancy discriminate against gender-nonconformant individuals who identify as alternatively gestational. In collaboration with the Church of Jesus Christ of Latter-Day Saints, the research concluded that non-conventional pregnancy can be traced as far back as the pre-inseminational stage, when unborn life pulsates like so many miniature miracles within the scrotal pouch. Thanks to these revolutionary discoveries, we were able to create The Abortion Avatar—and give Pro-Lifers the second chance that other people's unborn angels never got.

"How does it work?"

It's simple. First, our rigorously vetted donors provide fresh unborn issue at the vital post-ejaculatory stage. The issue is collected in the full splendor of its pre-youth in hermetic vials that preserve the sample at a cozy room temperature. We then select the right issue for *your* needs and ship it straight to your doorstep. Once delivered, The Abortion Avatar can be safely released from its encasing. And let the goo-goo gaga fun begin!

Stretch it! Fling it! Web it through your lover's hair! The Abortion Avatar is so easy to use, a twelve-year-old boy can enjoy it! It is even safe for consumption!

"It sounds expensive!"

Not for smart shoppers like yourself! With this one-time limited offer, you will be subscribed to weekly—that's right, weekly—batches of Abortion Avatar. Our unborn issue is locally sourced and obtained, and personally customized to meet your demands so that *you* can feel in control of your donor's body.

We even accommodate racial preferences. Hoping you could have changed that Latina's mind outside the clinic? Now, you don't *have to.* We'll deliver 100% pure Latino issue *to you.* Wondered what could have been of that Vietnamese couple's offspring? Wonder no more, because their fate can be in *your* hands. Literally!

Sure, life can be a mess. But we say yes to life. So say yes to the mess. Say yes to The Abortion Avatar.

9:55 AM

I'm not a fan of grandiose statements, so I will offer a self-evident universal truth. From time immemorial, man has questioned. In 2013, he asked what does the fox say. Earlier still, he asked what would Jesus do. If nothing else, I am a questioner. Just ask anyone and they'll tell you, "Did Bertram put you up to this? You tell that human laxative that he still hasn't returned my diaphragm."

And so, I pondered. And in my meditations on this lucid hallucination—this hallucidnation—called reality, I found an answer. I still don't know what the fox does say. I don't know what the Jesus would do. But I do know where a diaphragm does not go, and consequently, what the Greek pantheon would do and say if they were around today.

The answer was as contradictory and deceptive—as contraceptive—as oracular prophecy. It's on display in Aisle 8, between the Grecian cups and diva urns.

THE GODS OF OLYMPUS JOIN THE WORKFORCE

Since the fourth century AD, the Greek Gods have become increasingly irrelevant. Today, in this economy, they saw no alternative but to reinvent themselves in the job market to survive.

ZEUS PRIVATE INVESTIGATION

ATHENA: As your legal advisor, I insist you remodel the business, boss.

ZEUS: Behold, what sharper eye than mine to disrobe the secrets of men's bedchambers? Who nimbler than the Cloud-Gatherer to gather dirt off their "cloud"?

ATHENA: You've received multiple complaints from customers, and it's always for the same reason. Look at this one: "Assuming the form of a garden gnome to seduce a person of interest."

ZEUS: A satisfied customer, as I recall.

ATHENA: Her *husband* was the customer!

ZEUS: He suspected her of infidelity—and I proved him right. Another case deliciously closed by the mighty Thunder Rod. Behold, Grey-Eyes, have you ever lain with a rhesus monkey?

ATHENA: I'm your *daughter*, you pig!

ZEUS: I can assume that form, too.

HERCULES WASTE REMOVAL, INC.

MR. ERISTO: Jolly good, you're just in time. The groundskeeper was let go last week and, as you can see, Master's stables are in a frightening state of disrepair.

HERCULES: Hercules smash!

MR. ERISTO: Sweet Rhea Immaculate! What have you done? You've smashed Biscuit's head in!

HERCULES: Yes, Hercules smash.

MR. ERISTO: By Pan's whiskers, what is wrong with you, you brute? Master will terminate me! Oh, cruel iniquity! What shall I do? I have a wife and kids. Have you nothing to say for yourself?

HERCULES: Hercules smash?

MUSIC LESSONS BY APOLLO

APOLLO: Pray tell, young mortal, what vessel have you elected to channel the melodious epiphanies of the muse? The lyre, perhaps?

AXXL: Nah, homes. I wanna learn to *shred* on the electric guitar.

APOLLO: I see. And have you considered the lyre?

AXXL: Electric guitars are badass, fam. The hunnies will think I'm dangerous and rebel.

APOLLO: The women of Athens hailed me as intrepid and virile after I induced a thousand-eyed monster to sleep with my lyre.

AXXL: You're inducing me to sleep with your words, bruh! I wanna melt faces with my axe like Jimi and Angus.

APOLLO: Did I mention that the strings of a lyre are outstretched goat intestines?

AXXL: ...

AXXL: I guess that's pretty badass.

ARTEMIS HUNTING GEAR AND SUPPLIES

ARTEMIS: And how can I help you today, sir?

MACK TEON: Suppose I'm looking for camouflage gear.

ARTEMIS: And what will you be hunting, sir?

MACK TEON: Suppose I'm not so much hunting as prowling.

ARTEMIS: Prowling, sir? For what? Pheasant? Boar?

MACK TEON: Suppose I'm not so much prowling as prying.

ARTEMIS: Prying...

MACK TEON: Suppose I'm in the bush prying on some nymphs bathing. You got anything for that?

ARTEMIS: Suppose you were a stag, sir.

MACK TEON: What?

ARTEMIS: Suppose I sicced the dogs on you.

MACK TEON: I don't get it.

ARTEMIS: Start running, Bambi.

HEPHAESTUS BBQS AND GRILLS

HEPHAESTUS: I assure you, all our grilling equipment is certified volcano-to-yard and is manufactured using only the purest ore of Etna. Our laborers undergo extensive apprenticeships with the IBB in bespoke smelting techniques and satisfy all the requirements of the

Shirtless Blacksmith Act. Did I mention our scimitars placed second in Comicon's "Epic Blades That Are Not Andúril" contest?

HADES: I only came here to warn you that you'll need a real devil's advocate or there'll be hell to pay for those allegations of using blackface in your workshop.

HEPHAESTUS: Soot! It was soot! Our company celebrates inclusion and diversity!

HADES: Look, I'm just the messenger.

HERMES: No! *I* am the messenger!

DIONYSUS EVENTS AND CATERING

MADAME AGAVE: Don't get me wrong, the Maenad & Merlot package sounds wonderful. But are the naked flesh-eating women really necessary?

DIONYSUS: I'm sorry, I thought you requested a party. We bring the party. That's our motto. If you wanted lame and tame, you should've gone with Jesus H. Christ and Co.

MADAME AGAVE: It's a children's party!

DIONYSUS: Why didn't you say so? In that case, you're going to want to go with our Symposium Special.

DEMETER'S ORGANICS

DEMETER: Namaste. How can I help you, rugged sir or ma'am or gender-nonconformant war deity?

ARES: Meat! Lots! The tough stuff, for my men!

DEMETER: We actually don't stock brutalized animal carcasses in this boutique. But we do have vegan substitutes. Would you like to sample our farmstead meatless bacon? It's made entirely from reclaimed banana peels and onion milk. Our sumpweed-inspired decolonial chorizo is crafted in-house.

ARES: Hercules! Advance!

HERCULES: Hercules smash!

EROS RELATIONSHIP ADVICE HOTLINE

CALLER 1: My office crush won't notice me, and I've tried everything! How do I get him to like me, Eros?

EROS: Workplace relationships are tough to navigate. They require patience and can be vulnerable. Have you tried impaling him with an arrow?

CALLER 2: So, I have this friend—let's call him Paris. He likes this girl—let's call her Helen. He tried impaling her with an arrow and it didn't work! She's still married to her scumbag Mycenean husband!

EROS: Extramarital affairs are tough to navigate. They require patience and can be vulnerable. Has your friend tried abducting Helen and smuggling her to a foreign country?

CALLER 3: Yo, I been hustlin' to bed some shawties, but it's like they don't even notice me. It's like they don't appreciate how dangerous and rebel I am.

EROS: I see. And have you considered the lyre?

10:23 AM

In this multicultural day and age, when national borders are sliding doors for anybody with rolling luggage and a birthday, respectable establishments must be prepared to cater to customers across the spectrum: from local to global, patriot to cosmopolitan, and apple pie to strudel. And we are no exception.

But what about when the local goes global, the patriot expatriates, and the apple pie goes apple-bye? Our international best-seller has got you covered. Feast your eyes—or in the words of our seasoned globetrotters, "Esst euer Augen."

GRINGOS TRAVEL GUIDE: TIPS AND TRICKS FOR THE WANDERLOST INTERNATIONAL AMERICAN

ROME, ITALY

"When in Rome," they say. Here at Gringos, we say, "When in Rome, feel at home." And what's more homely than a fresh slice of za?

You may be surprised to learn that pizza was not invented in New York, but right here in Italy. And few Italians are prouder of their native delicacy than Romans. The competition for cosmopolitan pie connoisseurs is so stiff that they translate their menus into English—cue hilarious misspellings. ("Antipasti." Whazza big idea? We came to eat the pasta, not *oppose* it!)

Our choice of the best pizza in the piazza? Donatello's Deep Dish. You can't miss it: just look for the sign of the beloved Ninja Turtle. For the ultimate authentic experience, ask Luigi for a bottle of the locally sourced Trevi Fountain soda water. *Mamma mia!*

CARTA JENA, COLUMBIA

You've probably heard of the show Narcos. What you may not have heard is that it's based on a real country.

If your dream destination involves sandy beaches, pina coladas, and great deals, look no further than Carta Jena. The best part? The local flair comes to *you*! All you'll need is a towel and your wallet.

Take a load off on a rented beach chair ($8) and the world is your oyster ($12 for a dozen). Hail a local *muchacha* to braid your hair in the traditional style ($15). Flag down the *ceviche* cart and get your parboiled crab on ($10). Wash down the surf n' turf with an intoxicating (wink, wink) homegrown staple, like the classic Mojito ($6) or Cuba Libre (two for $10 before 6:00 pm). Don't forget to make your besties jealous with an original "Columbia: Magical Realism" tee ($30). Forgot your sunglasses? A vendor is never far away, offering original Bay Rans at bargain prices.

LONDON, ENGLAND

We know what you're thinking. "Pay a visit to our old colonial overlords? We dumped their tea into the ocean for a reason!"

Yet despite the language barrier, the British are quite similar to us Yanks—or as they pronounce it, "Wanks"—second only to the Italians. Like us, they enjoy Cheerios, so much so that they pay tribute to the brand after every encounter. They too find any sexual activity that isn't abstinence repugnant. And sure, they still treat their Queen like a beloved deity; unlike us patriots, who stopped making cults of personality of our political leaders. But they did get two things right. (Though dentistry ain't one of them!) The grub and the pub.

Conveniently, you can experience both in one sitting. Enjoy a pint of lukewarm ale while sucking on hard-boiled eggs coated in ground mutton, battered and fried, and keep those babies coming till you've "laid a brick in yer trousers," as the local saying goes. Or was it, "*you've* laid a brick in yer trousers"?

CANCUN, MEXICO

Ándale, ándale, ándale!—to Mexico, that is. Gringos' All-Inclusive Spring Break Spectacular remains our top-selling travel package, providing fun in the sun for our nation's most promising young scholars for over three decades.

Ride a *burro* on exotic excursions to Piñata Point and Chalupa Cove. See real-life *mariachis* perform such timeless Mexican folk classics as *La Cucaracha* and *Tequila.* Following the midday *siesta,* join the *fiesta* at Mexico's fifth largest Hard Rock Cafe—or as it's known in the local parlance, *Café Piedra Dura.* Gringos provides exclusive discount codes on unique souvenirs, like artisanal hand-decaled shot glasses and charming *sombreros* to "top" it all off.

Can, can, can *you* do the Cancun?

NEW DELI, INDIA

Gringos fun fact: did you know that, before there were American Indians, there were Indian Indians? Even more surprising is what these Indian Indians believe. Get this: they worship cows. (In 6,000 years since the creation of our universe, we are bound to encounter some ridiculous beliefs along the way.)

You guessed it. This makes it *very* difficult to find cheeseburgers in Deli, despite its misleading name. Luckily, we found the spot. Connaught Place is the place to cure homesickness, with H&Ms, TGI Fridays, and original Bay Rans at even cheaper prices than Columbia. And—yes—the classic hamburger.

Well, not precisely. In New Deli, the closest you can get to our all-American, definitely-not-German creation, is a Yak meat patty, topped with Yak cheese and a Yak milkshake on the side. Odd, yes. But as we like to say here at Gringos, "You can't spell *budget adventure tours* without *be adventurous.*"

TORONTO, UPPER AMERICA

For us Americans, the biggest difficulty of getting to Toronto is crossing the border. Fortunately, lax patrolling and commitments to naturalizing refugees have made it easier for us *personae non grata* to get in. Still, the local customs can be downright baffling to red, white, and blue newcomers. And we're here to help.

Gringos Toronto Travel Tip # 1: You may have heard rumors that Upper Americans don't pay for their healthcare. This is, sadly, true. We can only imagine what shoddy medical facilities that socialist policy has led to. We therefore recommend avoiding injury and sickness at all costs while traveling in Upper America.

Gringos Toronto Travel Tip # 2: If you were hoping to expand your collection of moose pelts while up in the Great North, you may want to rethink your hunting destination. AR-15s, M203s with *and without* grenade launcher attachments, and cruise missiles are not available for purchase—not at Walmart, not at all. Even acquiring a lowly Berretta APX means going through all sorts of hurdles, like background checks and wearing pants.

Gringos Toronto Travel Tip # 3. If you're Texan or Bostonian, Torontonians will be a particularly jarring culture-shock. Upper Americans will beg your pardon to get past you on the bus. In public, they speak at disconcertingly unloud volumes. Only a minority of them zealously parade their bipartisan loyalties. (In fact, their government has *more* than just two political parties. Do their sports also have more than just Home and Away teams? The mind boggles.) Worst of all is their dishonest advertising: Beavertails™ contain neither beaver nor tails.

Aside from these shortcomings, the trip to Upper America is worth it, if only for the poutine.

10:47 AM

When we first opened, our stock was not certified child-friendly by the CPS. So naturally, we became friendly with children. We were delighted to discover that they do indeed say the darndest things; not darndest-least of which were these little troopers' perceptions of themselves.

We attempted a look through the proverbial candy store window; but the candies weren't vegan or stevia-forward, so we had to conduct our research at the Confectionary Apothecary Farrier Lodge and Inn. The result? Top-shelf wares.

Literally. They're up there. On the top shelf.

NARS + LALS = YUM MUMS 4EVER

ECOLALIA: Hey Nars!

NARSSISA: Hey Lals! Consensual air hugs!

ECOLALIA: Are you also here to get curdled guano paste?

NARSSISA: Lals, I love you and don't mean to insult your life choices, but I read a headline the other day that guano paste adds phlogiston to your chest milk. They're now saying the best health boost for mommy-milky is oatmeal suppositories.

ECOLALIA: Ugh, I knew I shouldn't have trusted Chet's advice. You think he would've learned after the first pregnancy.

NARSSISA: Lals, I love you but the suffix "nancy" is a hurtful reminder of women's hegemony over childbearing. We use the inclusive suffix "roger" to subvert Western constructs that privilege the traditional holders of reproductive power.

ECOLALIA: OMG I am *so* sorry, Nars! I will def work on learning more about that important conversation. I'm just honestly really overwhelmed with the pregnancy—sorry, the pregroger—and all the hormones—sorry, the hormrogers—and it's just A LOT.

NARSSISA: I totes get it, babe. But you're, like, the strongest person I know. And I'm there for you, but also, I'm focusing on myself right now. Besides, you always have Chet and Lenux. How is Lenux, by the way? Has they chosen a gender yet?

ECOLALIA: TBH, he says he's a boy which is, like, bad. But also, I feel like he needs to express himself however he chooses. Does that make sense? I mean, he's five now. He's already doing peepee and poopoo in the adult potty. He's at that age when he can make those choices.

NARSSISA: Absolutes. Onyx is six now and she's *so* aware. The other day, she told me she was an astronaut and I had to call her Captain Onyx. So I wrote a letter to the school informing her teachers that her preferred pronoun was "Captain" so they didn't commit a microaggression against her.

ECOLALIA: That's, like, *so* brave of her. I also had to write the school because of Lenux. Can you believe they're saying challenging students is *not* a form of discrimination? It's like they never *heard* of alternatively-abled learners! I had to go to the Equity Resources Office to get an accommodation letter saying Len doesn't learn by homework or exercises or reading or writing, like cisnormal students. He has a unique condition that requires learning by techniques like rapid eye movement meditation in non-traditional learning settings, like grounds of play. It's like, hello, ever heard of disabilities?

NARSSISA: The situation at the schools is *very* concerning. The other day, Onyx told me that her consensual friend, Stylus, got peanut-shamed. He had to be sent home for the rest of the day to decompress from the trauma.

ECOLALIA: What the actual fuck, that's so problematic. When are those teachers going to take action to keep our children safe? We need to force the school board to make more diverse hires again.

NARSSISA: I'm proud to say that Onyx has risen up to institute change after the incident. She's leading her first petition! She's calling to decolonize the curriculum of Gandhi since he's at the root of systemic oppression against the otherly-histamined.

ECOLALIA: That sounds like a really important conversation.

NARSSISA: Yeah, everyone knows that Gandhi was an Elite Patriarch of the Caste System who, like, normalized concubinal abuse. And not only were his victims women of color, they were also anaphylactic.

ECOLALIA: That's, like, really problematic. You're very strong.

NARSSISA: I know, right? Speaking of me, can you believe I'm already in my second trimester? Hashtag canttell hashtag ironicnotironic! We're having a gender repeal party on Tuesday.

ECOLALIA: What's a "gender repeal party"? It sounds like such an important conversation!

NARSSISA: I saw it on Pinterest, it's *super* destabilizing of hegemonic patterns of oppression. You take the envelope with the ultrasound and, before opening it, you burn it because science is culturally insensitive and bio-essentializing. Oh my god, you should come! There's going to be swag bags with baby moon charts and Queefs4Palestine onesies! And bring Chet—but explain to him he's there to be silent and learn. Just don't tell Dels.

ECOLALIA: LGBTQ! What did Dels do this time?

NARSSISA: Her tweet yesterday was *very* offensive. She lost all this weight and said how she was "feeling great" and all this implicit fat-shaming stuff. And she used to be an icon of the macro-bodied community.

ECOLALIA: Eww. *Unfollow.*

NARSSISA: Hey, there's one box of oatmeal suppositories left! I would totes sacrifice them to you, Lals, but I'm in this place right now where I'm focusing on myself. Does that make sense?

ECOLALIA: Oh my God, yeah, no, of course, that's so generous. I fully support your self-care.

NARSSISA: Thanks, babe! Anyways, have to run. I have my garlic-custard enema in an hour. BTW, you should def try it. It's a five-month-long waitlist, but *so* cleansing.

ECOLALIA: You always have the wisest advice, Nars, I totes def will. Thanks for the important conversation, babe! See you on Tuesday!

NARSSISA: Consensual air smooches! Best to Chet!

11:06 AM

Do you take pride in the section of your dating profile that proclaims your love of a good book, supported by photographic evidence of tanned legs straddling a copy of Women who Run with Wolves? *So do we. We are, if nothing else, avid readers. Just ask anyone and they'll tell you, "I changed my phone number, my social media accounts—I even moved to a different tax bracket. Tell Bertram I'm filing a restraining order."*

Get pensive and camera-ready, dear patrons. Time to show the world how much you read.

FAMOUS TITLES: REJECTED DRAFTS

From *Moby Duck* to *Slaughterhouse-Pie,* your favorite page-turners as you've never read them before.

THE CATCHER OF THE STYE BY J. D. SALINGER

I strode the filthy Manhattan streets, aware in my surroundings of nothing but phonies. *"Poop"* and *"butt,"* I thought about those shallow pretenders. One passed me by, brushing my elbow with his smarmy falseness. *"Piss waffle!"* I yelled, shocking the phony witch-teat. There I was, authentic, amidst a field of baa-baa sheep. The field. I remembered the field, the words he sang. *I have something in my eye, said the catcher of the stye.* I had something in my eye, too, I realized. That poopy whore must have given it to me.

THRIFTY SHADES OF GREY BY E. L. JAMES

"Where did you get those sunglasses?" Anastasia interrogated questioningly.

Christian Grey's intoxicating stare studied her sumptuous frame, as the prurient bulge between his rugged thighs grew increasingly tumescent.

"I got them at a real bargain. Second-hand," he proffered nonchalantly. "I buy everything used," he aggregated grinningly, a coy smile elongating itself between his challenging cheekbones. The way his waxy lips pursed at the word "bargain"; the way his pearly eyes roamed, not entirely concealed by the dim lenses, and fixed hungrily on Anastasia's munificent bosom—it made the velvety walls of her unctuous pudendum tingle with spams of lustful abandon.

"Do you think you could get me a pair?" Anastasia squeaked blushingly, cheeks flushed a faint magenta, betraying moist appetite below.

Grey lowered his shades, his magnetic gaze penetrating Anastasia like a hot knife in clotted cream. His trouser-package aggrandized, as he naughtily enjoined, "I've got a pair for you right here."

MOBY DUCK BY HERMAN MELVILLE

Up on the deck, a delirious Ahab struggled to load the harpoon that would, he hoped, put an end to the unperishing obsession that had enslaved him to the briny deep.

"Over there!" cried Ahab, spotting a chiseled beak breaking the water. "Thar she breaches, the White Hen!"

"Quack, quack!" roared the feathered behemoth. "Quack, quack!"

As Ahab tussled for control over the harpoon, my mind took refuge in memory. It went back to that night at the Spouter-Inn, in what seemed a lifetime ago, where I dozed, deeper into dream, locked in Queequeg's interracial embrace. His name echoed in the empty space of my mind, sweeping me away from the brackish seaward madness surrounding me. "Queequeg. Queequeg." But it was too tenuous to hold; the name faded, smothered by the wailings of the Great White. "Queequeg. Queequeg. Queequack. Quackquack..."

HARRY POTTER AND THE CHAMBER OF COMMERCE BY J. K. ROWLING

Inside Hagrid's cramped hut, The Boy Who Lived paced nervously. Gringotts Wizarding Bank, Harry had learned that morning, was being audited. He stood to lose his inheritance money.

"What about an invisible ink potion?" spouted Ron; as usual, offering poor advice.

"Statements are the least of their problems," chastised Hermione. "These are muggle authorities, Ron. They're indicting Gringotts with muggle charges. 'Failure to transition from the gold standard.' 'Use of unrecognized legal tender.' 'Lack of approved PPE equipment in mine-shafts.' They're even being charged with failing to report the existence of mythical fauna."

"I'm going to have to sell my Nimbus 2000!" whined Harry, voice shrill and prepubescent. "I'm going to have to mortgage my cupboard!"

"Just because we can't use magic against them doesn't mean we can't outsmart them," Hermione rejoined. "To beat a muggle, you have to think like a muggle."

Her eyes darted toward the gingery mop-top. "Ron? Don't you have an uncle in Panama?"

GREEN EGGS AND SPAM BY DR. SEUSS

I do not like these, Sam I Am.
I do not like green eggs and spam.
These eggs are rotten, rank, verboten.
They're best if they were just forgotten!
They've sat in sun for days and hours.
They've sat while came and went the flowers!
And what's this side-dish of the course?
A can of meat of unclear source!
The dog won't eat it, nor the cat
—who merely stuffed it in his hat!
Zoonkles, zwonkles, zwig and zwack!
These spam and green eggs make me yak!
But if I'd drank a quart of rum,
I might kersplunk them in my tum.
Perhaps I'd eat green eggs and spam,
If I were hammered, Sam I Am.

SLAUGHTERHOUSE-PIE BY KURT VONNEGUT

Listen:

Billy Pilgrim has become stuck on thyme.

Billy has baked a pie with thyme-braised lamb in 1955 and has marinated veal in thyme ganache in 1941. He has poached quail in thyme reduction in 1989 and it turned out undercooked in 1910. He has made thyme three ways in 1912 and the same recipe yielded thyme à la king in 1850. He has seen the birth and death of many farm animals, prepared many pie crusts, and used many sprigs of thyme.

Once, Billy gave a whole platoon in Dresden diarrhea after feeding them thyme-glazed fillets of unspecified fish.

Sole, it goes.

FART OF DARKNESS BY JOSEPH CONRAD

"The infantile joke hung acrid in the air," continued Marlow. "Kurtz, his naked torso tinted by moonlight, had lost his sense of humor in those many years spent in the jungle's verdant constriction, a confinement mirrored only by the entrapment of his maddened soul. The paucity of laughter did not halt his juvenile routine. In this hinterland of wilderness, Kurtz alone marshaled comedy to its apogee, or so he was convinced. Back faced toward the silver moon, Kurtz beckoned the audience's silence, and let another one slip. A faint whistle issued forth, dissipating into the high canopies, and yet the stench persisted—noiseless, but lethal. Only this time, as the miasma struck Kurtz's nostrils, the fetid gag jolted him out of his fevered consciousness with a scream. 'The odor! The odor!'"

11:20 AM

I tried my hand at stand-up. In retrospect, it was unwise to try standing on my hand, so instead I dedicated a limited series to it. It's limited to one-liners, lined up in Aisle 1.

BITE-SIZED BITS

They say never meet your idols. I'm flattered. Nobody has come to meet me in years.

I ordered a rare steak at a restaurant. They brought me a collectible tenderloin.

Confucius was asked what it would take to change a lightbulb. He replied, "Many hands make light work."

"It's a bloody murder!" cried a foul-mouthed Englishman, identifying a group of crows.

I was told never to give up on my dreams. I haven't awoken since.

His son was named after his father. Naturally, since his father was sixty years older.

An apple a day keeps the doctor away. Especially if you aim straight between the eyes.

PETA's "Justice for the Whales" campaign made headway last month after invoking *habeas porpoise.*

He dreamt his mother had a wardrobe malfunction. His therapist deemed it a Freudian nip-slip.

The U.S. Supreme Court is ruthless. At least as of September 18, 2020.

A headline reported that the bicameral legislature celebrated the frozen rice porridge of a Central African nation's affable master of a party dance. It read: "Congress congratulates Congo's congenial conga king's congealed congee."

Humpty Dumpty's wife got laid by an egg.

I thought she was gaslighting me, but she later assured me I was only under that impression because I wasn't in my right mind.

A woodland wildlife sanctuary donated all its animals. They have no fox left to give.

If time were actually money, we would all be rich. Except for babies. Babies would be poor.

It's a bird, it's a plane, it's—possibly cataracts, my depth perception is a scandal.

If he wants to, the Englishman can rise to his feet and misplace twenty quid. He can stand to lose a few pounds.

The unqualified electrician didn't know this would be his last job. He was shocked.

You reap what you sow, and sometimes, you also rip what you sew.

Enola Gay performed at a comedy club. He bombed. An arsonist followed him. He had them rolling on the floor.

A proverb: "One in favor of words that describe actions."

A headline reported on the palpable absence of a Niagara Falls' attraction with mob ties. It read, "Made Maid of the Mist missed."

Though beggars can't be choosers, boozers can be chuggers.

A Dubliner climbed a Pole and wore a Thai, yet walked away Scot-free. Luck of the Irish.

The French chefs argued whether to prepare *civet de lapin* or *lièvre à la royale*, though by that point they were just splitting hares.

An American woman wanted to know whether there was a john on the bus, while a British woman asked if there was a loo on the lorry. It turned out that both John and Lou were on board. It wasn't long before they regretted identifying themselves.

A roaming Roman is an itinerant Italian, while a traveling Transylvanian is a roving Romanian. And a roaming Roman roving Romania travels Transylvania on an Italian itinerary. Romantic, right?

Does anyone know of like-minded people in my area? Asking for a friend.

11:49 PM

You must be wondering, "How do you do it, Bertram? How do you not get shut down by the Ministry of Labor?"

One word. Stay relevant: synergy, proactive solutioning, integrative multiplatform.

One word. Be bold: performative interconnectivity, enhanced data-cognizance threshold, fungible user-experience augmentation.

See for yourself. See your horizons, reenvisioned.

See this here? The See Monkey and Do prototype.

COMMENTATION NATION

Emote. Vituperate. Indignify. With Commentation Incorporated.

OUR VALUES

The cardinal truth at Commentation, Inc. is *vox populi, vox Dei.* And as the voice of God, we the people stamp out moral heresies, mainstream deception, and "expert" advice.

OUR PRODUCT

At a time of increasing difficulty in keeping up with the Joneses' online posts, it has become more urgent than ever to unmask the realities they are blinded from seeing. We all remember that day little Sally Jones shared a picture of chocolate ice cream that could be deconstructively interpreted as racist. But because you were too busy raising awareness about fetal personhood, little Sally's teachable moment was lost.

Thanks to Commentator®, you'll *never* lose those teachable moments again.

Streamlined for the perfect synergy of outrage and righteousness—or as we like to call it, Outrighteousness™—Commentator enables your true tidings to reach multiple users on multiple threads and chat boards, all at once.

Look out, Joneses! You're about to be *commentaught* a lesson or twelve!

OUR SERVICES

When you sign up with us, you'll receive a unique multiplatform handle, which ensures that all your truth bombs are easily and affordably dropped. Our unique algorithm allows you to cast a wide net. Using only a person's surname and active zodiac sign, we are able to track down their social media accounts, along with those of their friends, family, work colleagues, and dental care providers.

We value your privacy, which is why our unique subscription offers the full anonymity that the online community so sorely lacks, equipping you with a unique pseudonym and IP scrambler. And with our Platinum Pontificator Package, you'll receive a surrogate online persona, uniquely crafted in-house by our graphic design team to ensure that your identity is safe with us.

Once you've signed up, sit back and let your unique experience with the Commentator app begin. All you have to do is click the "Commentate Now!" icon—the app does the rest! Thanks to our unique JavaScript coding, the Commentator app can read *and reply* to users' posts at the drop of a bitcoin. With a growing digital library of over 300,000 uniquely pre-set commentations, ours is the largest automated opinion database on the market. And we know you'll love each and every one of them.

But don't just take my word for it. Take a look at these unique real-time replies by our Commentator handle.

OUR HANDLE

@SamO'RaisWord – Merry Christmas and Happy Holidays everyone! #hollyjolly #mistletoekiss #eggnogshart

Reply: @CommentInc – This ain't Agrabah, what "holidays" are you talking about, Sam? (If that is your *real* name.) This is a good *Christian* nation. Every year on December 25, we *Americans* bask in the glowing afterbirth of Our Lord and Savior, Jesus Heidi Christ. Take your liberal snowflake Inclusion Day back to communist Upper America. And another thing, by placing "Christmas" first and generically reducing every non-Eurocentric subaltern celebration to "holidays," you reassert White Male hegemony and commit vehicular manslaughter on traditionally disempowered communities whose yuletide performative expressions have been co-opted by neocolonial power structures. #MAGAmericaFirst #AOC&Omar2028

—

@MeyerMacCheyes – I went camping recently and got this rash on my legs, possibly from a dark green, broad-leafed plant. Any ideas what it could be and how I should treat it? Thanks! #WebMD #campingfails

Reply: @CommentInc – Have you cross-referenced your astral chart with the *I Ching*? Nostradamus predicted that the pyramids of Luxor and Cheops would align during the "seventh cycle of the seventh sphere of the seventh house." The C and O in "Cheops," the Roman numeral "V" which is two less than "seventh," the second I in "*I Ching*," and the D of "#WebMD" together spell 'COVID' (numerological value = 666). According to ancient Lemurian hieroglyphs, their year of $44.53X^7$, which conservative estimates put between the years 2012 and 2048 of "our calendar" (actually gifted to us by an exogalactic race), will enact a shift in *co*smic *co*nsciousness through a *vi*ral *vid*eo of penguins sneezing. That gives us: COCOVIVID. The 2017 Disney movie *Coco* is about life and death: *vida/vivido* and *muerte/muerto* in the Mexican vernacular. This adds up to: COCOCOCOVIVIDVIVID. Hope this helps, cheers. #OnTheRedPill #FreeMasonJar

—

@MarjorieTaylorGreene – Christmuss is UDNER ATAK from the JEWS of LEMURIA with there humongus SPASE LAZERS!!! #EdlersOfSaion

Reply: @CommentInc – Finally, someone says it like it is. Bumping and sharing!

OUR MISSION

With expanded character limits on X, increasingly sophisticated comments on Reddit, and the thriving of First Amendment rights on reputed alternative truth sources like TruthSocial, it is more important than ever to put your unique narrative out there. It is our unique mission to help your missionizing succeed.

So what are you waiting for? Join the Commentation Nation today and start smearing that unique awareness!

** Commentation Incorporated.
Make Your Voice Herd.™ **

12:03 PM

We all need a palate cleanser once in a while. My palate cleanser of choice is two thick slices of soda bread welded together by a slathering of peanut butter and melted marshmallow. Wash it down with a frothy pint of molasses and you're ready to tackle that fear of public speaking. A glass of ambrosia for the glossophobia.

But the food of the gods has been in short supply ever since our favorite imaginary deities ceased being salacious pranksters and were replaced by a stern father figure whose only son is a buzzkill. Thankfully, we made up for that loss with a franchise of dope superheroes.

We are proud to offer you those who did not make the cut.

HEROES AND VILLAINS: CHRONICLES OF THE B-SIDES

THE ADVENTURES OF TAXMAN AND ROBBIN'

Meanwhile, somewhere in the Cayman Islands...

TAXMAN: Drop the ledger, Evaderon! The jig is up. Your deductible days are over.

EVADERON: You think your vigilante justice applies here, Taxman? You're no match for my financial privacy clauses! Mwahahaha!

ROBBIN': Leaping lizards, Taxman! He's summoning his trust protector!

TAXMAN: All I want to know is why, Evaderon. Without a functioning taxation system, we are little better than animals. Besides, you're entitled to returns. Don't you miss those sweet, sweet returns?

EVADERON: You'd never understand my sinister motives. You know why? 'Cause you're the Taxman, yeah-ah, you're the Taxman.

ROBBIN': Baffling bandicoots, Taxman! He used that lyric without paying royalties!

TAXMAN: Have you no shame, Evaderon?

EVADERON: I'll tell you what *I* don't have—balance owing! And soon, my organization will be granted status as a religious affiliation under group ruling. You know what that means. Mwahahaha!

ROBBIN': Pontificating pangolins, Taxman! We've got to stop him!

TAXMAN: Let's get him, Robbin'!

Pow! Shwam! Audit! T50! Rebate!

ROBBIN': Lactating llamas, Taxman! The ledger is ours!

TAXMAN: Exemption denied, Evaderon. Don't you ever learn? In this world, nothing can be said to be certain except death—and *taxes.*

SUPERNAG

"Is that balaclava one-hundred percent cotton? You know you shouldn't be wearing polyester what with your eczema, Jonah. And Ezra, wipe that schmutz off your face! You're robbing a bank, not courting some *shiksa* at the discotheque! At least have some dignity in front of these *goyim.* No offense, Greg and Carl."

"We agreed aliases only! So much for concealing our identities."

"What's this I'm hearing? You're *ashamed* of who you are? Your grandfather crossed the Bering Strait wearing nothing but a tea cozy to migrate to this country so that you could rob banks, and this is the gratitude you show? Ezra! What did I say about that schmutz?"

"How many times do I have to tell you? It's *makeup*! I can't wear these damn polyester death-masks Greg brought—no offense, Greg—so I had to find another way to hide my face."

"Don't you take that tone with me! Why, if your grandfather were here, he'd give you a sound flogging with his tea cozy."

"Let's move! We only have a ten-minute window. We're wasting precious time!"

"Oh, so I'm wasting your time now? You weren't complaining about me 'wasting your precious time' when I was busy ejecting you from my cervical canal. I guess this is the thanks I get for prying the very milk carton from my mouth to calcify your growing bones. Which reminds me, Jonah, did you remember to pack a lunch? You know how you get after heists what with your hypoglycemia. I know Greg and Carl made sandwiches, but they're bound to contain porcine traces. You know how these *goyim* can't go a day without their bacon—no offense, Greg and Carl—and what with your proneness to anaphylactic shock—"

"Umm, guys?"

"What Greg!?"

"The bank is closed."

SNAILMAN

"Help! Someone, please!"

"Fear not, citizen—"

"He's getting away! Get him!"

"For it is I—"

"He's gone! And he's shot that poor woman!"

"Snailman."

"Quick! She needs medical attention!"

"What seems to be—"

"She's losing consciousness!"

"—the urgency?"

"Oh, cruelty and despair! She's bled out. It's over."

"All in a day's work for—"

"Ma'am, come with us. We have a suspect in custody and need your help identifying him."

"—Snailman."

AFIKOMAN: THE BAKED CRUSADER

A bounty on his head. A warrant for his capture. A search party out for gelt. Under thick of Seder night, our hero lies concealed in linen closets, lodged behind armoires, stashed under tablecloths and sofas. He sees all, but none see him. They smell his presence, yet detect him not. The only one who knows his location refuses to betray the Afikoman. Who will be the next to *pass him over*?

CAPTAIN BUZZKILL AND THE FRATERNITY BOY

"Bruh, there's a catfight at Pier 69 we should totally break up."

"You know the protocol, Julius. We address cases in order of priority. At this moment, the Felony-Finder is showing an act of perjury being committed at a Small Claims Court. That's a criminal offense. To the Tandem Bike Mobile!

"Drag dude, can't we take the Party Chopper for once? And don't call me Julius, bruh, it's so lame. Call me J-Hawg, like my bruhs do."

Later, at the Small Claims Court...

"Whazzup in this court, bitches? Which one of you bitches is perjuring up this biatch? Don't *make* me whip out my Rod of Truth."

"What my associate means to say is that we have it upon good authority that a punishable offense under Article 9, Section C-46 of the Criminal Code has been carried out in this place of jurisprudence. We are here to identify and apprehend the perpetrator while minimizing use of force."

"Let me at him, bruh. I'm jacked. Hold me, bruh. Hold me."

"See, this is the reason I advised against imbibing that Red Bull and Jägermeister on the way here. It impairs your judgment and over-stimulates aggression. Folks, we will proceed in an orderly fashion to interview each witness. No stone will be left unturned until justice is served."

"You'll never catch me alive, Captain Buzzkill and The Fraternity Boy!"

"There he is, yo! He's making a run for it! Let's tear him a new asshole!"

"For once, I concur with you, Fraternity Boy. Let us pursue the culprit and mutilate his bodily frame until he has acquired a secondary anal chasm. To the Tandem Bike Mobile, Julius! Or should I say, J-Hawg?"

THE SOVIET STINGER

"Vell, Mr. Bond. I see you half found my secret hive. I suppose you sink I am—how you say?—'like fly stuck in ointment'? Little did you know your associate, Miss Chestalot, vas *honeytrap*! Tie him up, Svetlana!"

"Relish it while you can, Dr. Melissov. In about fifteen minutes, MI6 will have this lair surrounded."

"Zer you are mistaken, Mr. Bond. You see, my organization and your government have been—how you say?—'in cahoots' dis entire time."

"Poppycock! The Queen would never!"

"So innocent, Mr. Bond. Did you ever stop to consider that all along your precious Queen vas—*cagey bee?*"

META MAN

Meta Man arrived on the scene, awaiting the author's instructions as to what to do next.

"What nemesis will he have me face this time?" Meta Man asked himself. "Does he even know yet? Or is he masking his lack of ideas for a narrative plot with this internal dialogue?"

But upon further reflection, Meta Man wondered, "Or is *this* the plot? Is this internal dialogue, this mere text occupying the page, itself the plot? And are my reflections on my thoughts being part of the plot *themselves* part of the plot? And, God forbid, are my reflections on my thoughts being part of the plot being themselves part of the plot an even *further* part of the plot?"

Meta Man realized this meditation could continue spiraling *ad infinitum*. He broke it off then and there to avoid bashing the reader over the head with tediously bottomless self-reference; a tendency his alter ego, David Foster Wallace, was so notorious for. Instead, he resolved to return to the first narrative layer. "Author!" Meta Man called to the author. "Hand over the plot!"

"But I already have," said the author, writing himself into his own narrative. "Or have I?" he then added. "After all, if I am here, who is writing *me* into the narrative? And what *is* the narrative?"

"Mind. Blown," said Meta Man.

Or did the author have him say that?

Or did the author have the writer write the question of whether the author had him say that?

And is the author the writer, and the writer the hero of this story, namely, Meta Man, all at the same time and yet none at no time?

"Mind. Blown," said the author, as he stared at the narrative he had just written, which he would seek to publish one day in a collection along with his other short pieces. Such as this one.

12:26 AM

Perhaps it is the acrid sting of day-old bedpan assaulting my throat and eyes talking, but one of you is in desperate need of alone time in the water closet. The lavatories are on your left; I ask that the responsible party make constructive use of them.

As for the rest of you, if you'll follow me to this next section, you'll see the latest in paying homage to the literary greats.

"How now, my liege?"

I'm mirthful I enquired. Saunter to yon wares, sirrahs, and avaunt from this putrescent fecal mist.

THE BARD EMBALMS THE TOWN IN CRIMSON

Never mind how, but The Bard was able to afford an apartment in the city.

He split the rent, to be sure, though more than once he'd had to cover Chinaski's portion. The Bard had contemplated asking Chinaski to leave for good this time, but he dreaded the conversation, especially since he was unlikely to find his roommate anything but indisposed due to his constant intoxication.

BARD: *(Aside)* Courage, mine heart! Resolution, mine spleen! Let not the bile of contumely pollute my reproach, but that it be swift and just. Hal, thy terminal moment is nigh. Forth from this domicile shalt thine legs pallbear thee, an if thy lips refuse. Perished is the hour of clemency, the last syllable of thy implorations hath its potency forsworn. Hie thee hence, and find thine haven 'neath some other fool's eaves, for this fool shan't another eve don the coxcomb.

Thus sized-up, The Bard strode purposefully down the hall, ready to confront Chinaski. As usual, he found him in the tub—his fifth bath that day—staring at nothing in particular. Scattered ash dotted the tiles around the empty champagne bottles he was using to deposit his cigarette butts.

"Three for the price of one!" Chinaski said, gesturing to the bottles and suppressing a burp. "All I had to do was subscribe to some monthly bridal bulletin. I used your card; they're still refusing to approve my line of credit. That's Democrats for you. Background check this, indecent exposure that. Anyway, they'll start charging you after the second month."

BARD: How now, sirrah? Wouldst pilfer my identity, and impawn it to squander a farthing? 'Tis a fetch too far! Thou takest me for a pliant rustic, Hal. Alack, here expires the abuse! Some other accursèd soul shall the crucible of thy cohabitation shoulder, for mine own spine shan't another round of Helios's chariot abide thee.

"Cut the drama, Will," Chinaski said. "You're no roommate of the year yourself. Who in the hell is gonna put up with your constant babbling? And those little monologues of yours—you think I can't hear you? I'm standing three feet away! Just because you break eye-contact with me and stare out into space doesn't mean you're inaudible all of a sudden. To say nothing of the cross-dressing. That's right, pal, I'm on to you. I've noticed the missing panties in my Chest of Triumphs, and I know for a fact it isn't their proprietors who snuck back in to reclaim them."

Defeated, The Bard stormed out of the bathroom. Once again, Chinaski would have his way.

"Besides," Chinaski yelled from down the hall. "If it wasn't for me, you'd be sinking the flesh-torpedo even *less* than you already do. Which reminds me, it's Tequila Tuesday at Bottoms End. Girls drink free—you know what that means. Get dressed, we're going out.

The Bard acquiesced. At least Chinaski was good for one thing.

—

Chinaski wore his usual slacks and t-shirt, unlaundered both. The Bard sported his dark green breeches, ruffled shirt, and codpiece. He also wore his suede jerkins in case it got cold.

They entered Bottoms End and sat at their usual table.

"Quadruple bourbon," Chinaski told the server. "Make that a double. And put it on Will's tab."

"And for you?"

BARD: Prithee, barkeep, enumerate for me the libations enoaked in yonder casks. I wish to unparch my palate with a more refined vintage than this rude abutting chaperone.

"We've got ale and pilsner," said the server.

BARD: A frothy quart of ale, vixen, tut tut! Ah, to anoint my tongue with amber brew, 'tis ritual old, but each time new!

Every time these two clowns showed up, the server thought, one of them managed to get himself thrown out. She wondered who it would be this time.

—

"What do you think of her?" Chinaski said, a few quadruple whiskey doubles later. The girl, Chinaski figured, was the right kind of androgynous to satisfy The Bard's kink. "Chicks like confident men, Will. And if you come across as anything in that queer outfit, it's confident."

The Bard was suitably inebriated by this point. And so, liquid courage coursing through his veins, he made his move. He approached the damsel Chinaski had pointed out, and attempted courtship.

BARD: Sublime enchantress, an if it please, mightn't I laud thee with a sonnet, the which, though nor justice nor propinquity to thy countenance can offer, will perchance a lone step toward the vault of thy graces ascend. Thou blush'st? Why only fairer doth it make thee! 'Tis the scarlet kiss of Dawn upon thy cheek. And like her sun, thy bosom riseth with each palpitation of that heart for which mine own I'd fainly offer, and on my very sword fall but for a sojourn in thy tender embrace. Yea, madame, those portly crescents of thy chest do my loins ensorcell—and quite another thing cause to rise withal.

"You're funny," said the damsel. "What's your name?"

But before The Bard could answer, in charged a beefy man; a seasoned pugilist no doubt, thought The Bard.

"You talkin' to my girl?" said the beefcake. "I'll kick your ass, fag!"

But The Bard, determined to defend his damsel's honor, confronted the beefcake.

BARD: She, a flower *thine*? Pshaw! And how hast thou swindled this unblemished maid into thy company, rogue? By what churlish sorcery hast behexed her into thy favor? Displays of gaud and ornamentals? A motor carriage of ostent and expense—to conceal the lacking girth of thine manhood, no doubt. A pox on thy baubles! I shan't allow swine like thee to cast themselves afore this pearl!

"What did you call me?" said the beefcake.

BARD: Unstuff those ears and hark closely, vile slop. Verily, I'd pluck thine beard, if thou hadst one on thy vulgar maw! Thou leper's toe! Thou bowel's sneeze! Thou art no man, thou art a melon, into which my rapier I will heartily plunge, to mince the insides and leave thee for a buzzard's banquet. Fie, cur! Avaunt and be gone, back to the squalid crag whence came'st, and tarry there till grimly Death cleanses this earth from the accident of thine birth.

But before The Bard could unsheathe his rapier and deliver on his threats, a security guard came at him from behind, put The Bard in a headlock, and lugged him toward the exit.

BARD: Unpaw me, ruffian! I shalt escort mine own self from this strumpet's den! Howbeit, not without first prying yon spritely maiden from the talons of that engorged jackanape. Abscond with me, bewitching beauty! Come forth, gentle lilac, and let us clinch our carnal union.

To everyone's surprise, the damsel followed. Out the two went, The Bard and his dame, with Chinaski staggering behind.

"See you two loveturds at home," a legless Chinaski slurred, emitting a small parcel of vomit with a burp. "If you need me, I'll be in the bath. And Will, get more of that champagne on your way back, they don't allow me in the more anystore. What's this country coming to when every time you accidentally drop your pants while admiring a bridal bulletin? I'll tell you where, craight in the strapper, that's who. Damn Democrats."

BARD: *(Aside)* 'Tis the very prurient hour of night
anon this bawdy bard's delight
will into his bedchamber steal:

an offering to his lustful zeal.
This bodily magnificence
will yield to his concupiscence
and with his spade shall he unflower
his newfound Helen and with power
shall he resolutely claim,
"Pronounce my name, thou filthy dame!"

"Hello?" said the damsel. "I'm *right* here. I can hear everything you're saying."

Exeunt omnes.

1:06 PM

The best part is you can add made-to-fit suede jerkins to this model if you sign up for our monthly bulletin.

"What bulletin is that?" I may be asking.

You can find our sample issue on the counter beside the cash. And don't mind the coffee stains. Yes, that's what they are. Coffee stains.

THE CONTEMPORARY CULTURE REVIEW

The refuse are in!

Rating scale
☹ = Triggering
☹☹ = Microaggressive
☹☹☹ = Problematic
☹☹☹☹ = Offensive
☹☹☹☹☹ = Fascist

DR. SEUSS (1904–1991)

It triggers the mind to think that a whole generation was brought up on the systemic discrimination of Dr. Seuss. This should not be surprising: the title "Doctor" is an exclusionary signifier that marginalizes subaltern medical practitioners, like crystal healers and physicians of the Church of Christian Science.

As a gender-fluid druid, I am uniquely affected by Seuss's dehumanization of non-traditional fantasy characters. His use of mythophobic slurs, such as "ooblecks," "glikkers," and "diffendoofers," is especially genocidal. Seuss's narratives champion cisnormal heroes, like Cindy Lou Who, who is not an otherly-abled Whovillian of color. Though his work contains subtle stereotypifications of Chinamen and Orientals, it is most disturbing for its validation of anti-trans attitudes, betrayed by the failure to celebrate Yertle the Turtle's subversion of genitocentric anatomy.

I do not like this Doctor man, he should be placed under a ban. I do not like his bigot ways, he's clearly phobic of the gays. He makes up words that don't exist, we zees and zirs this Seuss resist. And worst of all, his ham and eggs—I disemboweled them on my legs.

😟😟😟😟

THE QUEEN'S GAMBIT (2020)

As a member of the rook-presenting community, I am uniquely affected by a show that capitalizes on a cultural appropriation of the Ancient Persians: chess, decolonially known as *shah mat.* That the protagonist, despite the misleading identifier "Queen" in the title, is in fact a white non-genderqueer woman, adds post to trauma.

Faithful to its supremacist agenda, in every match the *white* pieces go *first.* And what does defeat look like in this imperialist normalization of violence? In losing one's *king*: aka, in a threat to patriarchal power structures. By failing to equally prize all players for participation, this show serves as shameful endorsement of meritocratic elitism. Why does everything have to be about "winning," aka, domination of the disenfranchised?

This show *could* have been an important step forward though much remains to be done, had its focus been on the closeted cowboy character and his journey of identity.

😟😟😟

J. K. ROWLING (1965–JUNE 6, 2020)

It may shock you to learn that the author/ette of Harry/iet Potter was once an icon of the LGBTQA2I^{nth} community. Her pseudonymous gender affirmation as Robert Galbraith, followed by the de-affirmative reversal back to J. K. Rowling, was the high-water mark of identity performativity, second in bravery only to Judith Butler's deconstruction of graphemic expressions of andrological biopower in the Western sexualic imaginary through Derridean hyposemiotics.

Prior to her betrayal, Rowling gave a voice to the struggles of liminal characters like Hermione Granger, who as a half-blood not only destabilized the witch-muggle binary, but was long read by hyposemioticians as the doyenne of anti-Voldemortian dialectics. But on that hateful day, blinded by menstrual rage, Rowling posted the Tweet-That-Must-Not-Be-Named. In it, she discursively genocided the validity of witchcraft and wizardry for extra-fictional assertions of ovulation in non-biofemales.

As an auto-declared ovulational non-biofemale, I am uniquely affected by Rowling's bigoted reinforcement of the ovulation gap, which systemically excludes members of the performative menstruation community by its privileging of "estrogen" and "cervixes." If wands weren't symbols of phallocentric supremacy, I would use one to cast a disapparating spell on Rowling—and I am *not* jk.

☹☹☹☹☹

COVID-19 (CRYPTOZOOLOGICAL FAUNA)

The Patriarchy reached its hegemonic summit in 2020, when even nonliving organisms internalized their prejudices in the form of COVID-19. As a self-identifying airborne entity, I was uniquely affected by the pandemic.

The virus disproportionately harmed communities who chose to live their truth over the metanarrative imposed by protofascist institutions of power like hospitals (see Foucault, *Birth of the Clinic*). More problematically, priorities in protection against the viral cryptid skewed immeasurably in favor of first-responders, aka, of the Privileged, who were handed on a silver platter the opportunity to dedicate years of study and effort to medical expertise.

But the most postcolonial aggression of the mythic virus by far was toward the macro-bodied community. By targeting body-shamed "obese" folk, it doubled their likelihood to be hospitalized as compared to anti-dysmorphic weight-conformant folk. The genocidal fat-profiling was only made worse by COVID's bio-essentializing tendency to be harsher on pregnant women, rather than equitably targeting *all* folks who identify as pregroger, making it plain that the virus had read J. K. Rowling.

☹☹

THE SUN (4,600,000,000 BC–5,000,000,000 AD)

It is no wonder that the label "the Sun" was constructed by Caucasian males in positions of power. Who else would impose the assumption that its pronoun is "the" and not "they"?

This act of metatextual violence explains why the heat is described as "oppressive": the Sun is complicit in Western astronomy, which invalidates the lived experiences of alternative cosmologists and predicters, like augurs and haruspices. As a dowsing rod, I am uniquely affected by this silencing of my truth. Last but most offensive, the Sun is responsible for illuminating visual markers of distinction, like gender and race. Next time you witness a Privileged exercising his implicit bias, you can blame the Sun for enabling the visibility of Otherhood.

In this dowsing rod's opinion, it is time we told the Sun that it's *lights out.*

☹

THE CONTEMPORARY CULTURE REVIEW (1988–PRESENT)

Textual signifiers cannot embody my lived indignation against The Contemporary Culture Review. As a rook-presenting gender-fluid druid auto-declared ovulational non-biofemale airborne dowsing rod, I am uniquely affected by this phallopatriarchal heterofascist cisbourgeois dialectical genocide. The author of this oppressive discourse believes that beliefs are a laughing matter—I therefore advocate oppressing the oppressor. Take *this*: ha! And *that*: hee hee! And also *this*: hardy har!

How do you like how that uniquely affects *you*? Opinions are like pinions; which in your opinion, it is funny to clip. Well, clipple me this. Get me the manager of this rotten review and prepare to be subtweeted out of employment! The only way to cancel a cancer is by canceling it.

Power to the people! Silence is violence! You are either with us or against us! The revolution will *not* be televised! Now think outside the bun, silly rabbit, Trix is for kids! Can you hear me now? Good. Cancel my subscription to The Contemporary Culture Review, and while you're at it, cancel yourself. Yabba dabba doo. I am the Batman.

☹☹☹☹☹

1:24 PM

This is one of those counterintuitive facts, but certain things cannot be captured in headlines, posts, feeds, memes, or even GIFs. We call such things "things."

A thing, as we all know, is an old Nordic tradition of collective decision-making. And like all great Norse traditions, it involves long undercuts, braided beards, and a rugged gluteus maximus. So plant your gluteus maximus down for this special presentation, while I drag my own G. M. to the backroom to enjoy a long, steaming coffee. Yes, a coffee.

And worry not, intrepid patrons, Jo will take over from here.

Bertram out.

OUT TO LUNCH

BERTRAM'S EMPORIUM OF THINGS PEOPLE SAY

The *Body Positive* aisle in Bertram's Emporium makes you feel like Hunter S. Thompson at a Pride Parade on mescaline. You walk across it and a motley chorus of buzzbotz is set off by motion sensors, programmed to intone jubilant self-worth buzzlinez in swift succession. You hear the evergreen classic, "You're beautiful just the way you are!" Or the hymnic, "My body, Jesus's choice!" And such reprised anthems as, "We're here! We're queer/bi/tri/demi/semi/pan/trans/glans! Get used to it!" The botz are encased in some of the racier shells of the Emporium. Conspicuous among them is an inspired array of dildos ranging in size from moderate to moray (featuring electroshock stimulation), the "Thicc AF" line of assless chaps (also available in jackfruit leather), and the signature "Brazen Brassieres," with all skin tones and areola circumferences equitably represented. And that's not the half of it. You've got your Moravian gimp's branding iron, your Afghan anal marmalade, your Tasmanian dual orifice Peg-Master 9000, your Barbary Coast prostate thwacker, and for the vanilla, vanilla-scented scalding wax. To the untrained eye, it looks like the sex shop in a Mormon nightmare. But Bertram's is not a sex shop. Bertram's offers products that sell better than sex. Bertram's sells ideas.

Okay, "ideas" might be too strong a word. Bertram's sells what you might describe as condensed ideas, like the taglines of an idea. Except not all buzzbotz offer taglines of ideas either. Some are popular adages while others are more like slogans. And not all are body-positive.

There are as many genres as there are aisles at Bertram's. Aisle 4: *Spiritual Wisdom* (Dalai Lama and Eckhart Tolle one-liners). Aisle 9: *Counterculture from Punk to Crypto* (Naomi Klein and Elon Musk fans alike). Aisle 11: *Cosmic Love* (the New Age section). Aisle 6: the ever-popular *420 Friendly Philosophy.* There is *Killer Comebacks* on Aisle 13, *Fratboy Frases* on Aisle 5, *Street Slangs* on Aisle 2, *Street Smarts* also on 2. In fact, there is so much variety that the only property shared in common by all of Bertram's wares is that they involve things people say.

And yes, that description is not very informative. The store's original name, slightly more informative, was Bertram's Emporium of *Shit* People Say. But Bertram reasoned that such gratuitous expletives might dissuade the more strait-laced clientele, such as Mormons. He failed to realize that all it takes to repel Mormons is coffee, tea, booze, and unmagical underpants. They might appreciate the non-monog botz, though.

And okay, yes, I keep referring to these "buzzbotz" and "buzzlinez," which I have provided no explanation for, throwing you into the story *in medias res.* But fear not, you will know what they are soon enough—it would be artless of me to just *tell* you. After all, there are few clichés less forgivable than a glaringly obvious set-up for exposition; with the one exception of those tedious metatextual tactics for breaking the fourth wall, such as addressing your audience directly. As the studious literati out there know, that rhetorical device immediately betrays an unreliable narrator endearing himself to his audience. You can rest assured: I am not that kind of narrator and this is no attempt to endear myself. There simply is not enough at stake here for that—this ain't *Lolita.* This is not about me or the nymphettes I court by the poolside. It is not about calling me Ishmael and skirting my strongly implied same-sex interracial liaisons. This is about things people say. It is about the Emporium that sells those things. And, most importantly, it is about the people that buy them.

1

"This place is *so* random," Femme Teen 1 says to Femme Teen 2. "It's so random we just *walked* in here."

Bertram repairs a dysfunctional buzzbot behind the cash belonging to the KKKaren series. The electronics board, a tangle of wires resembling the unbalanced chakras of a frustrated Karen at a PTA meeting, juts out of the inverted bob hairdo shell. The words, "Call the manager before I diarrhea on your floor!" spew out of the blonde encasing. The voice is a robotic baritone, about two octaves lower than it should be, and with overly long decay. Bertram glances at the teens.

"Look at this one!" says Femme Teen 2, referring to a *Fratboy Frases* original issue featured in the storefront. Bertram had recently been tinkering with its buzzlinez. The label on it reads, "Gender Studies Chet."

Femme Teen 2 activates its command button: a ping pong ball afloat in the silicone beer foam that tops the red solo cup shell.

The beckoned bot responds in its characteristic Jock Drool # 3 voice-setting: "That female-presenting server totally consented to banging me last night after setting clear boundaries!"

The Femme Teens look confused. Either that, or their eyebrows are done to resemble a permanent state of confusion.

Femme Teen 2 presses the command button again and the bot speaks. "Bruh, talking about emotions is gay, which is a perfectly acceptable lifestyle choice whose visibility we should increase and celebrate."

It looks like the Femme Teens have had enough of Gender Studies Chet. They make towards the cash counter.

"Ohmygod, do you *see* the rando behind the cash?" says Femme Teen 1, in deliberate earshot of Bertram.

"Is it super random if I think he's kind of hot?" says the other. "But, like, in a random way?"

In the drawer beside Bertram is a Flitting Valley Girl buzzbot, which Bertram has been updating with the hottest trending buzzlinez. It is shaped like a smartphone housed in the Ironic Hot Pink case, eerily like that of the Femme Teens. Bertram whips out the buzzbot and hails the teens to the cash.

"Did that rando just call us? This random is *so* random."

"Do you want to see something *really* random?" Bertram says, displaying the hot pink buzzbot. "Check this out."

He taps the command button.

"This place is *so* random," says the buzzbot, in pitch-perfect likeness of the teens' tinny monotone.

The Femme Teens look consternated. Either that, or their eyebrows are done to resemble a permanent state of consternation.

"Ness, this rando's a toxic masculine," says Femme Teen 2. "Let's go. This situation is making me feel really vulnerable, and *not* in a random way."

"Hey bucko!" says Ness. "No means no! Unless you are deconstructing the systemic oppression of yes/no binaries."

Bucko. That particular term of address, coming from the likes of these ladies, takes Bertram by surprise. Despite the so random word choice, he retaps the command on the Valley Girl bot. "No means no!" it says in tinny monotone. "Unless you are deconstructing the systemic oppression of yes/no binaries." He would have to modify it to include the "Bucko" line.

The Femme Teens look pissed. Either that, or their eyebrows are at it again.

"You've done it now," says the one who isn't Ness; unless they both go by Ness, which is a possibility Bertram has not yet discounted. "I'm Discording about this place's unsolicited sexual advances and predatory behavior!"

"Oh dear—" says Bertram.

"Oh dear is right, bucko!"

"—I just realized this is not the one for you. *This* is the one for you."

Bertram whips out KKKaren, inverted bob hairdo exposing a tangle of wires, resembling the Femme Teens' own tangled frustration. The teens move from threat to suit.

"You'll be hearing from my lawyer!" they shriek in chorus.

Bertram can't help himself. He activates the bot. The Femme Teens huff out of the store to the fading sound of a robotic, long decaying baritone: "—hearing from my lawyer!"

What's another seething review anyway, he thinks. Let them have their fifteen characters of fame.

2

"You know the policy, Jo," says Bertram. "I can't accept returns if the buzzline is no longer in circulation. And according to my charts, the last popular uses of 'Fo shizzle ma nizzle' were registered in 2014."

"It's coming back," says Joanna. "Coming like a mule's engorged semen-rocket, Bert. I have a sixth sense for these things."

"For one, mules are famously sterile, so their seed literally bears no fruit. For two, that's exactly what you said about 'P-H phat' making a comeback. Now I've got a surplus of unsellable Frosted Tips Skater Boyz gathering dust in storage. I tell you what, I'll give you half-off on Corporate Douche 3.0. This model is never out of fashion—the trust-fund hippie crowd keeps it afloat. God only knows what they use it for, probably as a voodoo doll to hex with anti-capitalist incantations and aromatics. Which reminds me, I just received a shipment of the latest Trust-Fund Hippies. This series features zany new buzzlinez like, 'I'm discovering how cleansing it is to let go of work and bills' and 'I didn't just receive this blessing. I impregnated the universe-mother with my intention.' They're available in glossy- and matte-finish singing bowl shells."

"You know," says Joanna. "I bet you could push Corporate Douche botz on those pseudo-anarchist protesters, or for that matter, on pretty much any effete humanities student in an institution of higher education. They all deeply resent their parents for becoming cogs in the oppressive machine that pays for the Banksy decals on their iMacs and their degrees in professional complaining. I bet you would run out of stock within the hour if you opened a pop-up on a university campus."

"I can see why hippies with disposable income are fond of them. Same reason the original hippies singlehandedly boosted the VW Type 2 in the '60s: ritualistic necessity. But what makes you so certain that the overeducated vanguard outragees will be as receptive? They're not interested in anything that isn't shareable, likable, or bumpable."

"Because their own rituals are all about ironically embracing irony to an extent that makes it serious. According to the subaltern mathematics of their universe, two ironies a sincerity make. Hence, ironically buying Corporate Douche botz to make an ironic statement against capitalism. Why do you think their young millennial forerunners bought Anonymous masks to protest corporations? It's not like they were oblivious to the fact that Warner Brothers directly profited off those sales—well, maybe some were. But that's not the point. Their point was the same as that of their current Gen Z protégés: to vindicate Andy Warhol. And what better way to do so than to turn protest itself into pop-art? It's Warhol on post-ironic steroids: the artist and his art are eliminated because the people are simultaneously art and artist. It's the ultimate height of pretension embodied at the lowest level of the literal streets, akin to smoking a Cuban cigar in a portable shitter."

"I guess I haven't given it as much thought as you," says Bertram. "But now that you mention it, I have sold a few Corp Douches to punk rockers before. Despite what the ideals patched on their backpacks suggest, they don't seem too bothered by the fact that the electronics are made in a factory in Shanghai owned by an American multinational that is the farthest cry from anarcho-syndicalism. Not that they ask. They just ask if it's okay to retint the botz in neon green spray paint or would it damage them."

"There's reason to my madness, Bert. Aren't you going to reward me for that valuable nugget of marketing wisdom? How about an East Coast Van Lifer bot to go with the Hippie?"

Joanna has been coming to the shop for some years now, and if she's proven anything, it's that her various gambles on upcoming trends are like finding the exit in an Escher painting: the direction seems right, yet she always ends up back where she started while Escher's popularity is *still* on the wane. On the other hand, her drive to keep a finger on the pulse of contemporary culture is genuine. Her reasoning is often sound, even when she misses the mark. Besides, the trend industry is like that, beset by the kind of uncertainty that plagues the quantum universe and the recipe for street meat. This whole business is a gamble anyway. Joanna just needs a second opinion once in a while to help her hedge her bets more intelligently. Not to mention, he is going to need a prospective heir sooner rather than later. The thought of wizening his way till dusty death somewhere near Aisle 14 (*Dietary Advice You Never Asked For*) crosses his mind often, and it petrifies him. If there is anyone who cares enough about the shop to keep it going, it's her.

"How about a job instead, Jo?"

3

It's two days since Joanna started working at the Emporium and Bertram is already regretting his decision.

"I really think we should move Flat-Earth Frankie to the counterculture aisle," she says. "It's less of a fringe clique than you think. You'd be surprised how many people wade in that bog of yeasty shit. The whole conspiracy is propelled onward like a shart-javelin by anti-establishment motivations. More than a few of your Trust Fund Hippies and Chemtrail Charlies are parties to that whole flat-earth hollow-moon Lemurian messiah horseshit."

This is the eighth or ninth rearrangement Joanna has suggested for the shop. She means well. But if this goes on, the shop will end up looking more like Bertram's Emporium of Things People Move.

"Everything you have said on this matter, Jo, adds up to a suggestion for creating a new aisle dedicated solely to conspiracy theories."

As soon as he has voiced it aloud, Bertram realizes the suggestion is not as flaccid as he originally assumed. The idea of taking on that massively annoying task might occupy Jo's compulsive reordering.

"You can't really call it a 'Conspiracy Theories' aisle, Bert. That name might draw in enthusiasts in that purely ironic-not ironic-yes ironic sense. But you would be alienating the customers you really want, which are the honest-to-Xenu conspiracy theorists. There is a bigger market for people who want to hear their opinions validated than for those who want to ridicule those of others. Sure, the comment sections on social media are cataracts of disembowelment, but those are mainly troll-on-troll bukkake circles. There is no real profit in disagreement when what each user ultimately gets off on is exhibitionism: exposing their erect voices to the world and seeing their words reflected back at them. The old echo chamber cliché: except it's more like a hall of mirrors where each is jerking off to their own reflection and licking the surfaces afterwards. My suggestion is to brand the conspiracy section something that says acceptance and celebration of their viewpoints instead of demeaning them. Something like 'Real Truths.' Yes, that would work."

Bertram doubts he can take many more of these lectures. Joanna does have a point, but it's too early and there is not enough caffeine in his system to enable him to decipher what that point is. I need another coffee, he thinks, and opts for the path of least resistance, giving Jo the green light to go along with whatever it is she is suggesting. Something about a chamber of mirrors where trolls go to masturbate.

"I trust your judgment, Jo. Just one thing before you get started. Be a dear and fetch me a double-shot cappuccino. Not from our machine, it's on the fritz. I need you to go out."

Bertram realizes this is a good excuse to have some Joanna-free time. While she's at it, he can get her to dip her toes in some fieldwork. Win-win.

"And Jo? Take that notepad with you. Consider this your first buzz-gathering assignment. Pay especially close attention to the statement-people. You know the types. You can always count on at least one barista to don full identity gear. The heavily tattooed ones with Van Dyke beards and frames that look like they were welded by a frontier blacksmith are usually a safe bet. Also, be aware of any visibly self-categorizing clientele. These would be the petit bourgeois yoga moms, the flamboyant foodies, those tweed-clad bespectacled lesbians who think neutering their male pets is an act of anti-patriarchal subversion. Make sure you go to that café on the Ossington Strip, The Silk Tampon Room. It's a goldmine. On a single afternoon there, I once spotted no less than five twenty-somethings sporting "Girl Boners for Shariah" crop tops and "Hot for Hezbollah" keffiyehs, who looked like if they spent a single afternoon under the midsummer Lebanese sun their skin would flake off in large chunks of translucent parchment. For cultural contrast, I'll send you to a greasy spoon in Parkdale next time. There's one that is practically the headquarters of meth-addled ufologists and Qanoners."

Jo beams at this entrustment of responsibility. She says, "Aye, captain," and leaves the shop with a sailor's salute.

—

While Jo is off on assignment, two power-suited businesswomen enter the shop. They look quite young and quite successful, like they carpet-bombed their way up the corporate ladder and scorched everything and everyone in their path. Perhaps that's equality: increasingly more women thriving in traditionally male-dominated workplaces, where moving up is conditional on cultivating your sociopathic traits.

The two also look as if they're going forehead-to-forehead in the tightest ponytail competition. Bertram wonders whether he could pitch them a Strong Independent Woman bot. He is about to go fetch one from the back, but on second thought, they look like the type that takes vocal offense to a male showcasing a product he thinks they might enjoy, as if to imply that the one thing women are good for is shopping. He decides against it. It's too early to be righteously dumped on.

"How can I help you two?" Bertram says, prudently stopping himself before adding "lovely ladies." The ponytails approach the counter. One of them flashes a business card.

"We represent National Konscience Viral Distributors," she says. "Do you have a moment?"

"I've never heard of you," says Bertram, examining the business card. The card cites the following credentials in bold typeface: "PhDs in Problematicity and Grievance Studies."

"Actually, you have," says one of the ponytails. "Or you should have. It was our buzzline samples you received two weeks ago. The ones that were *meant* to be uploaded to the Pussy Power prototype, which we *also* sent. Except we didn't see that prototype in the storefront, as the sampling package requested. It may not be legally binding, but they're free samples for crying out loud. You could have done us the courtesy."

"Look, I appreciate the samples. It just seemed to me that they were better suited to a different bot. Better for the intended effect I was going for."

"Which is *what*, exactly? To trivialize important conversations? To defecate on social activism? Sure, let's just leave the genocidal status quo the way it is, it doesn't need subverting. After all, *your people* benefit from it. Hell, you're probably one of those neofascist neanderthals who want to return to the status quo ante, back when your group's power was truly uncontested. Where's your MAGA cap and Grand Wizard hood?"

It looks like being righteously dumped on by these women is Bertram's lot today.

"First of all," he says, "how could I wear both a cap *and* a hood? Spatially, that does not make sense. Second, it seems to me that you two are doing just fine in this unsubverted status quo. The way you are decked to the nines in Bay Street regalia is not a convincing plea for welfare, ladies. As for 'my people'? I know we all look the same to you, but my people are the Jewish people, and the status quo ante for us is Treblinka and Auschwitz, Nuremberg Laws, pogroms, ghettos, inquisitions, blood libels, crusades, and Augustinian witness doctrine. And victimhood was not even in fashion back then. We Jews had to overcome by becoming usurers, Hollywood executives, and reptilians. So, unless there are any further virtuous assumptions you would like to champion, you two ponytails should make like demonic possessions and return from whence you came. And take your Pussy Power botz with you. The craftsmanship is shoddy and well below par. They look like Kirby's botched lobotomy."

The ponytails, rather than looking positively suffused with indignation, look oddly pleased with themselves. In fact, they are smirking. And he had managed such a wistful comeback, too.

"Clap, clap, clap," claps one of them, invoking the slow-clap cliché. Then she says, "There's that cocky rando who thinks he's such a smooth humorist with his sarcastic barbs. Listen closely because I'll only ask this once. Take my buzzline out of your offensive Valley Girl bot and put it in my Pussy Power!"

"I'd like to put something else in your—," goes through Bertram's head, before it dawns on him. The ponytails, no wonder they look familiar. Familiar like the *Femme Teens*! Time to go medieval on their stiff asses. He would pull Strong Independent Woman bot on them.

Femme Ponytail 1 stops him. "Before attempting whatever little stunt you're thinking of pulling, I want you to reflect carefully on your last abusive encounter with us. Ness remembers. Don't you, Ness?"

"Like it was yesterday, Ness."

"That makes two *survivors* of your toxicity. Not ringing a bell? Your unsolicited advances? How you degraded us when we said no? Does your mind need refreshing? Because if it does, I have it all written down in my hot pink cellphone, right here in this text box, ready to post. And yes, I do have twelve million followers, not to mention all the influencers our company employs. All I have to do is press 'Send' and you can wave your present and future employment goodbye, bucko."

Bertram reads the accusations, condensed into 280 damning characters: *"... deeply traumatic misconduct ... the toxic masculine who runs the store ... triggering rhetoric of phallic domination ... implicit incorporeal rape ... carnal sin in thought ... justice for us survivors."*

"None of this is true!" says Bertram.

"True?" says Femme Ponytail 2. "Wake up and smell the matcha, Grandpa. This is the post-truth era. If this gets out, your little novelty shop will be canceled faster than you can say 'due process.' And *I'm* due processing releasing this post right fucking now. You feel me?"

Bertram knows this number. He knows how it ends, too. He is no superhero, after all: he can't avoid the daily masochism of reading the news. It's over, he thinks. Over like Blockbuster. Over like Pluto's stint as a planet. Over like Apu on The Simpsons.

"What do you want?" he says.

4

Jo gets back with the coffee and Bertram sulks. The Femme Ponytails have just left. They'll be in touch, they said.

"Bert, I can't wait to show you my buzzlinez harvest! I shit you not, I think I collected enough to start a whole new line of Julius K. Hipster botz! By the way, who were those intense ponytail chicks? I saw them leaving the store. They looked like their faces were being lifted by their hairlines. Are they the models for the Corporate Douchette series? They're *perfect*, Bert! Bert?"

"Jo, just give me a moment. I need a moment."

"What happened, Bert? What did those women do to you? I swear to God, you tell me where they touched you, Bert. You tell me, I'll knock the hairlines clean off those wispy cunts. Haul those slenderwomen back here, I *will* introduce them to a galaxy of torment."

"Jesus, Jo, nobody touched me. Hand me my coffee. And go back to therapy. I'll explain."

Bertram recounts the episode with the Femme Ponytails. It is a tale of Bay Street douchettes and reptilian Jews, of barbs and comebacks, of revolting falsehoods and heinous accusations. A tale of matcha-guzzling grandpas, of defunct Blockbusters, of Pluto and Apu, and most importantly, of blackmail most foul.

"These are the products they are forcing us to beta-test and eventually sell," says Bertram.

He passes the National Konscience Viral Distributors catalog to Jo. The acronym "Nat Kon Vi Dis" is inscribed in glittery characters on the front cover.

"Can you believe this tepid smarm of shit?" he says. "Look at these shell specs. Right there. The left column details the buzzlinez they plan on assigning to each bot. Look at this Pussy Power miscreation. 'My struggle. My truth. My world. As I prefer it.' They must have taken that line straight from a text penned in a Munich prison cell in 1924. And you know what else? We don't need to bother with hiring voice actors for the recordings anymore because *they* will be supplying them. How generous! Veritable Mother Teresas, these conniving twats. Except, as you can see, the contract also stipulates that we are obligated to allot 45% of the sales floor to their new merchandise. Which means we have to liquidate a metric fuckton of our older *and current* inventory at a profit about as modest as Mother Teresa's drinking habits. And that's only on the condition that we don't end up losing money because of this. Oh, but we can keep the Body Positive botz, Allah be praised. They're *big* fans of those. Despite that whole generation's tiresome façade of blasé irony, they still fail to recognize it when it stares them straight in the face like a famished owl contemplating lunch.

The rehearsal of recent events stresses out Bertram as much as the events themselves. He's going for a smoke, he tells Joanna. She'll come with. But just as they are about to leave, a wiry character waltzes into the store, erect as a cornstalk. This does not portend to be a customer they can just let peruse the aisles to his heart's content. It is evident from this patron's constipated gait and flatiron expression that he comes with no intention of perusing. No. As suspected, he is here for quite loftier purposes. He is here to interrupt their cigarette break.

"Aha, are you the proprietor of this establishment?" says the cornstalk man.

"And you are?"

"Aha, very well. I anticipated you might pose that particular interrogative. I have prepared these here printed surrogates of my verbal reply. Aha."

Cornstalk presents his business card. Right Morals Viral Productions, it says. Splendid, thinks Bertram. Fucking splendid.

"This concerns me how?" says Bertram.

"Very well. You see, my company—," he begins. His jittery eyes dart towards Joanna, like the pupils of those nocturnal monkeys that resemble a permanent amphetamine overdose.

"Forgive me," says he. "It was unmannerly on my part to neglect the lady's presence, overzealous was I to conduct my business. My salutations."

He tips his bowler hat to Joanna. Yes, he has a bowler hat, which, yes, he tips. Joanna stands there, debating whether to laugh at this man or boot him in the taint.

"And now, if it is quite agreeable to you, the men will conduct commercial intercourse. Does the lady need escorting to the adjacent room? Or will she guide herself there unchaperoned?"

"The lady stays," says Bertram, moments shy of Joanna booting Cornstalk in the taint.

"Aha," he says, putting on an expression suggesting accidental loss of rectal virginity in a bus stop. The short hairs of his pencil mustache slightly bristle.

"Very well, if the gentleman gives his blessing. You see, my company, that is to say, the business conglomerate that I represent, it endeavors to stay abreast, as such enterprises do, of the maneuvers and deeds of competitors. In the course of surveilling these adversaries, we found that one in particular presents an ongoing antagonistic front to our mercantile efforts. It so happens that the rivaling league in question has in very fact, not two hours past as the cock crows, approached this locale of vending, not unindubitably with the intention of negotiating a compact betwixt the concerned parties. Is this a faithful account of that engagement, sir?"

Merciful Amun-Ra, I'm going to kick this dandy in the taint, thinks Bertram. He rubs his eyes and holds off punting Cornstalk between the legs.

"There is absolutely no reason for me to disclose that information to you."

"Yea, to be sure, no such reason would there appear to be, verily and in point of fact. Yet there is, as I will now propound, compelling incentives in lieu of it. In any event, you would not, should you opt to asseverate, betray any details that we are not already aware of. I extend a courtesy to you, sir, for I know that emissaries of National Konscience did, not two hours ago as the cock does crow, approach and moreover enter these shop grounds, having therewith proceeded to initiate transactions with you, the proprietor, who did, subsequent to that oral exchange, ratify a written agreement with said emissaries. Whichever the offer they put forth, we, that is to say, the company I represent, are prepared to meet it, and even, within limitations, commit to top it, pending, it must be noted, strict guarantee by the signatory party that they, which is to say, our obstructors of competitive monetary advantage, remain incognizant of our arrangement, as stipulated in this here clause of nondisclosure. Aha."

Reining in his first impulse to force-feed this man his own bowler hat, Bertram realizes there may be opportunity here. The gutter deal with the Ponytails is guaranteed to lose him money; just liquidating old stock would bleed him dry. Besides, nearly half of the sale profits on their products were slated for National Konscience anyway, and they intended on returning only an insulting fraction to cover overhead. At least Cornstalk was offering an actual deal. At a minimum, he could cut his losses. If he's smart about it, he could even turn a profit. All he has to do is keep the Ponytails in the dark. 55% of the store is still his to stock as he sees fit: he would offer Rig Mor the same 45% that Nat Kon had usurped. The remaining 10% would be for original wares until someone folded, or ideally, both of his new partners and their companies, that is to say, the conglomerates they represent, imploded. It was a simple matter of making sure the left hand did not know what the right one was doing. Schedule their supply vans on different days. Same for when they insisted on meeting in person. As long as he could ensure that the twain never met, this arrangement might work, at least long enough for the respective clientele of the rival companies to become fixtures of the Emporium—at which point: the classic bait-and-switch. Until then, he had nothing to lose but his chains from this *laissez-faire* pact.

"We will discuss this in the back," Bertram tells Cornstalk. "My colleague will show you there. Joanna?"

Joanna stares at Bertram in disbelief. Unless the idea is to show him to the back with the actual intention of sawing this butthole's thumbs off, Bertram has lost his marbles. You know these Right Morals lunatics, she expresses with a glance. This goes against everything this place stands for, Bert.

"Show the gentleman to the backroom, Jo. I will join you shortly."

Joanna grudgingly ushers Cornstalk to the back. She turns to Bertram, her expression saying, this is a joke, right? We are only taking him back there to waterboard him.

But the reply on Bertram's face does not confirm that reading. All it says is, I need a smoke before returning to talk with this beshitted clown.

5

"I hope you're happy," says Joanna. "Now we have *two* ludicrous catalogs on our hands and only 10% of the store remains for our own products. And I had creative ideas, Bert, ones that would have turned this place around."

"I don't like this any more than you do, Jo. But I didn't have a choice. At least this way our assess are not entirely owned by those National Konscience thugs. Now they are evenly spread between sworn enemies; who, I am hoping, will end up at each other's throats over this until they both choke. This may seem like an impetuous decision to you, but it is not. Once the Emporium becomes the battleground for Nat Kons and Rig Mors, the two forces will cancel each other out, like Quaaludes and Adderall."

"Have you *taken* Quaaludes and Adderall at the same time? Because I have, and if that's the analogy you are going for, be prepared for a delirious disco night of the soul punctuated by bouts of rage and euphoric incontinence. Mind you, in hindsight, it seems unwise to have parachuted those benzos."

"What is your point?"

"My point is that this is a volatile cocktail, Bert, and one that cannot help but end in a violent case of the runs all over the linoleum. Did you read these Rig Mor Vi Pro brochures? Look at this one: 'Rigged Election Rick comes in two options of unique, all-American shells, expertly crafted by legal taxpaying patriots like yourself. Flaunt your shining national pride with the Fourth of July Hamburger shell. Or, if you've got that stiff Yankee Doodle for Second Amendment rights, the Red White and Blue AR15 shell is the one for you.' We don't even celebrate the Fourth of July here, to say nothing of their make-believe gun laws. Who the shit is this even meant for?"

"If you're concerned about a lack of customers for the Rig Mor products, you can rest easy, Jo. It's a short skip and a jump northward for our 'merkin brethren to come hither to the land of milk and syrup to enjoy our legal weed and their nativism. There are even a few of our own nationals—right and left, and cynical both—who like to pretend that we are on the same sinking ship of madmen that they are in. So don't worry your pretty head, you can always count on a crowd for this market. Rabble culture is, as ever, America's top export."

"I don't know, Bert. This whole thing stinks to high heaven like bacterial vaginosis. It goes against everything we stand for."

"Respectfully, Jo, this place is mine. I started it. You work for me, and this place was never meant to 'stand for' anything. Leave 'standing for' to the customers. Because at this moment, and in light of recent bullshit, my only objective is to keep this place stand*ing*. If you are willing to help me do that, superb. If not, you can clear your locker, no hard feelings."

The first tangibly uncomfortable silence between them descends like the Hindenburg crash on mute.

"Forgive me, Bert. Bertram. I'm here to help."

"Good. You can get started by moving these boxes of Gender-Fluid Fannys to Aisle 2. Everything to the left of Aisle 7 is for Nat Kon products since Body Positive is already in Aisle 1. Everything to the right is for Rig Mor stock. As for Aisle 7, we can make that Real Truths since it is where most of the overlaps are. Once you are done with the Fannys, we have got the Mar Tay Greene Gospelers going to Aisle 9—on second thought, make that Aisle 7: they make sense alongside the Rob Ken Jr. Jockstraps. The Q-Anne-Aunts and Boycott Berthas are going to Aisle 3, Deplatformed Dons to Aisle 10, Free Falestine Farrakhans to Aisle 4, and Fellowship of Thoughts And Prayers to Aisle 11."

Joanna silently gets to work. She lifts the box of Gender-Fluid Fannys, and a few go off inside the box. A series of muffled "Decolonize pronouns now!" and "Say zer name!" buzzlinez resound. Bertram calls out again as she makes her way to Aisle 2.

"Joanna," he says. But he realizes that it makes no difference at this point, and that only platitude could appropriately capture their reality. It is what it is, and they are where they are. "Never mind."

A final muffled "Grammar are colonialism!" is emitted from the box. It is the last "sentence" to pass between them that day.

6

Bertram arrives at the Emporium later than usual following his two successive meetings, one with Cornstalk, the other with the Nesses. He hauls in the new additions to the Emporium. This is it, he thinks. This is what it feels like to sell out. Perhaps there is no avoiding it: everyone sells out to someone or something at some time. Metallica. Nirvana. Hell, even Gandhi sold out. That's probably not true. Did Dr. King ever sell out? Wait a second, what's up with that sign?

"Joanna," he says. "Why is that section in Aisle 3 called 'Hollywoke'? It's supposed to say, 'Wisdom of the Stars.'"

"Because," Joanna says, "even if *you* don't believe this place is about something, *I* do. Besides, this is not getting in the way of your precious plans. I stocked everything exactly as you told me to. But I thought we needed some rebranding precisely to uphold our contracts with those soul-sucking harlots and that dickless fop in good faith. I think our customers should be able to know exactly where to find the botz that complain about the unrivaled bigotry that systemically plagues the awards shows that movie stars throw in honor of themselves. And the thing is, 'Wisdom of the Stars' doesn't quite capture that. I was going to call it, '*Hollywood you Keep your Acting for the Movies?*' but the sign wasn't big enough."

"I see what you are doing, and it needs to stop."

"I am merely thinking about how I can make it more convenient for customers to navigate the new shop grounds."

"Right. But in another, more obvious sense, you are trying to save face because I have become the poster-whore of Big Culture. But as that whore, Joanna, I have to keep the pimps paid and happy, at least until business is hot enough to force the two to royally fuck one another out of relevance. Until then, we need to pretend that we're obediently falling in line like the owned bitches that we are."

"At least hear me out, Bertram. This sign thing: it seems trivial, but it's a small gesture to preserve a semblance of our former dignity amid this fecal tornado. Besides, I was not being disingenuous when I said it would be good for business. The youth only understands ironese, right? So, I wrote a sign in ironese. Proclaiming yourself 'woke' these days is a badge of honor, not a term of abuse. Or if it is, it has lost its potency due to overuse, and hence pretending to use it as a term of abuse is now in itself ironic."

"Fine, keep your sign. But just one thing, Joanna. Do not go behind my back again. The next time you think of doing something like this, you run it by me. As long as it does not threaten the peace with Nat Kon and Rig Mor, I may even allow it. I assume this is not the only one?"

"Now that you mention it."

"Show me the others."

"It's all Zen, boss, I haven't written out the signs yet. Not all of them."

Joanna opens her notepad to the page with her new ideas. The proposed changes include:

1. Tits for Tat. "This one would replace the *Free the Nipple* sign."
2. Dead Babies No-Jokes. "*Fetuses 4 Life* section. Obviously."
3. Reclaiming Sexual Predation. "This is for the *What's Good for the*

Gander is Good for the Goose series."

4. God Hates Nags. "For the *How-to Guide for Christian Wives* line."
5. All Sex Is Rape. "That one's for the *Lesbian Leviathan* limited launch."
6. Close Encounters of the Yid Kind. "This is for the *Beware the Zionist Space Lasers* limited series."
7. Ku Klux Kops. "Believe it or not, for the *Defund the Police* section."
8. White Frivilege. "This here is for *Inclusive Rebranding of the Color of Snow*."

"These are clever," says Bertram. "I'm okay with 1-4, 6, and 8."

Joanna blushes.

"Give me some credit, Jo. I'm not an irredeemably uptight asshole."

"Not irredeemably. And thanks, Bertram. Bert. Thanks, Bert."

"Hey, let me ask you something."

"Shoot."

"Did Dr. King ever sell out?"

7

Only one week has passed since the recent overhaul of the Emporium and business is booming. Which is good, right? Sure, I sold my soul like hot pants in June, but it's not like I had a choice. Besides, what change was I bringing about before this fiasco anyway? Listen to me. *Change.* When was changing *anything* ever part of the plan? Changing what? People? People don't fucking change. The only thing that changes is fashion. And the fact that people are hardwired to follow it, like sea turtles pilgrimaging to spawn, is an immutable law of nature. Either that, or they follow the leader. They follow the leader, leader, leader, follow the leader, like that asscrack dance song from the '90s. How did it start? "Da roof is on fire." Christ, what an awful song. The late '90s and early 2000s were a dismal epoch for music. Remember the Vengaboys? Hell, the Vengaboys don't remember the Vengaboys! I wonder where they are now. On second thought, I do not wonder that. That wonderment has not once crossed my mind, not once. But if I had to venture a guess, it would be that their bloated corpses are washed up on some rocks off the coast of Ibiza, which they sang about in that one song, seagulls pecking at their toes while their glowstick bracelets are still dimly aglimmer. "Aglimmer." Is that a word? Who cares? It's not as if I'm ever going to use it. "Adventitious." Now that's a word I would like to use.

These and other such thoughts occupy Bertram's inner dialogue as he works the cash. His elbow rests on the counter and his chin rests in his palm.

"I'll take who's next," he says.

The call is meant for the next customer in line, even though he hardly *intends it* in her direction. Before even focusing his eyes on the person, he has already run a complete identity scan. The store has seen more than a few patrons of her background and phenotype since the recent launch of new stock. Educated middle-class youngbloods with income to dispose of and awareness to raise. This particular iteration has located a crowd favorite to dispose of said income on: the A Is For Activism buzzbot. Technically, this model is designed for the age group for whom the eponymous children's book is meant. But it has proven a hot ticket among the apostolic undergraduate armada, probably because they have the emotional maturity of children, judging by how quick they are to throw temper tantrums until they get their way and force an unsuspecting professor's expulsion on grounds of misgendering them. Bertram swipes the item across the barcode reader as the bespectacled tweed warrior reaches for her credit card.

"These make particularly good alarm clocks," Bertram says. "They're designed to a*woke* you." Tweed Warrior seems sold; even though, for Bertram, that quip lost its luster about fifty repetitions ago. She poses for an ironic selfie with the new purchase, to which an ironic caption will be added the likes of "their designed 2 a*woke* u lol."

"I'll take who's next," spouts mechanically from the cashier.

The curious thing about the Emporium in this new permutation is the comingling of social types, which has become all but forbidden in any other context, save perhaps ballot boxes. To be sure, they stick to their aisles. Only the more eccentric of the lot cross paths in Aisle 7, and occasionally even cross swords there, too: many a LARPer and cosplayer frequent that section. Interactions are rare, but there have been some. One time, a tinfoil-hat survivalist talked chemtrails with a crystal healer. Turns out the one's commune is just down the road from the other's bomb shelter. On another occasion, a gun-toting libertarian bonded with an unbathed youth who called himself an anti-statist and an anarchist, failing to register the redundancy of that self-description.

But by the looks of it, Tweed Warrior is not about to engage the specimen goggling behind her in the line. And sure enough, she all but walks *through him* as she makes her way to the exit, so engrossed is she by her new buzzbot; though she also seems partly driven by a mission to ignore this person out of existence. The ignored specimen is of the downhome blue-collar genus: the sort that the Tweed Warriors of yesteryear would have been able to identify as proletarian, and through some unaccountable alchemy of the mind, thereby identify *with*, despite not having worked a day of their lives in a factory or having lifted an object heavier than a hardcover of *Das Kapital*. But the Tweed Warrior redux of today is not concerned with class as a category of oppression. It may not have bothered Marx, Engels, or Lenin that their firmly bourgeois class status prevented them from claiming *their own* oppression while speaking on behalf of the oppressed; but these days, lacking a claim to victimhood amounts to social suicide. Luckily for her, she happens to be a "her," and a plausible survivor of anxiety or fat-shaming at that. As for the queueing blue-collar crewcut male, he suffers from the additional curse of being several shades too pale to register in Tweed Warrior's mental spreadsheet of folks who are allowed to have had tough experiences. But to be fair, Downhome looks none too keen on making this liberal snowflake's acquaintance either.

"That will be $67.79 after tax," says Bertram. Downhome pays cash for the Rebel Yelp buzzbot. Another popular item, this buzzbot is outfitted with stark raving excerpts from online forums of the deep hinterwebs, such as: "Say no to autism. Say no to the syringe," "If the globe is warming, how come I'm so cool?", and "A cabal of pedophiles is *not* a minor issue!" Such nuggets of wisdom are now his for the low, low price of $67.79 after tax.

"This here's the last one, too," says Downhome. "A gift for my Ma's fittieth. Was hiding way's back there in the Deep State Nine section."

"It sounds like an adventitious find," Bertram says.

Having used that word in a sentence gives him a small joy. Alas, like the current fire in his soul, it too is only dimly aglimmer.

8

Yesterday, Joanna reports, Trinity Bellwoods Park was abuzz with buzzbotz. As in, parkgoers physically brought them along, in droves. So commotional was the atmosphere that it led to a buzz-off. A gaggle of inebriated slackliners pitted their Weed Warlocks against a platoon of Pectoral Patrix, of the Sportz Studz series. The winner of the buzz-off was unclear and, it seemed, it was the failure to declare a victor that provoked the ensuing scuffle to break out. (Not between the botz, between the people. The botz are not programmed with belligerence activation functions.) This eventuality seemed all but fated, says Joanna, since the ratio of buzzbotz to tallboys was one-to-six: nary a dry throat in sight. This being Bellwoods in summer, the CP24 van was not far away. They dutifully captured the melee and ran it on the six o'clock news, after which a local blog caught wind of the buzz, so to speak, and published a two-minute read earlier this morning labeling Bertram's the city's "Best Kept Local Secret." Which can only mean one thing, Bert. Expect a crowd today.

No sooner than Joanna makes the ominous prediction, a queue materializes outside the shop, like sharks corralling prey. The consumers are ravenous for the hot baubles, identity brimming in their eyes. Cornstalk and the Nesses are bound to storm the shop today as well. They are not going to be pleased, Bertram realizes. Just recently, Cornstalk had expressed his discontent with the "rising tide of blackamoors on the premises," arguing that he feared such ethnically visible clientele would devalue the perception of their joint venture in the eyes of his more desirable God-fearing demography. As for the Nesses, they were guaranteed to throw a hissy fit about the white privilege of the now-viral Pectoral Patrix botz and their bimbo-shtupping high-five hot takes. To hell with it either way, thinks Bertram. Cornstalk, that is to say, the company he represents, is bound to disagree with Nat Kon regardless of the subject matter. Nat Kon could advocate gay conversion therapy tomorrow and Rig Mor would oppose it solely on principle. No matter what Bertram did, the two archnemeses would see no alternative but to deke it out and, Jove willing, obliterate one another in the process.

"If you build it, they shall come," says Bertram, gazing on the multiplying mass outside. "Open the floodgates in five, Jo. And announce 30% off all series marked with the radicalia label. You know the ones I'm talking about. Commie Comrades, David's Dooks, Femme Fashistes—both the Sarsour and Mallory models—as well as Antebellum Nostalgia. Make sure the mayhem is caught on video and post it. It's time to Black Friday this motherfucker into the ionosphere."

The mob has morphed into a horde by the time Joanna opens the Emporium. In spills the horde like molasses through a funnel. It is a motley ooze, concentrated at first in the entrance, then forking out the further it flows in, its various components sorting themselves into the aisles, like levees diverting a single stream into many tributaries. The situation is immediately volatile, a powder keg ready to go off with the faintest spark of provocation. And provocation comes soon enough, in the form of a young creationist refusing to accept that Noah allowed trans people on his ark.

"Two of every animal! *Two!* Not three, not 'other,' not 'prefer to not disclose'! 'Male and female created He them, sayeth the Word,' says my Jehovah's Fitness buzzbot. And 'the Word comes straight from the Father, through the Holy Ghost, and out the Son,' my Christ Crusader says. Preach! 'The Father is the ventriloquist, the Son is the puppet, and the Holy Ghost is the ventriloquist's hand.' No, that does *not* sound like God fisting Jesus! God hates sodomites, He would never! God only wishes to shower his children with love! Don't you wish to bathe in the

Lord's golden unction of love?"

It does not help that the young creationist's interlocutor in this particular encounter is a screeching bulletin board of identity categories. "As an infrasexual post-pubertine Chicanex victim of anxiety and depression, I find your narratives triggering and problematic. For one, my Judith's Butler buzzbot teaches that there is metatextual evidence of God's performative subversions of gender binaries in deconstructive readings of the Book of Hosea. Second, the invisibilization of gender-nonconformant fauna in Biblical times is responsible for the fact that they are not registered as having boarded Noah's Ark, but that is only because they were segregated from the cis-gendered ruling majority. You really need an important conversation from my Hackademic Heloise buzzbot."

It isn't long before supporters amass around the disputants. But unlike the confrontation at Trinity Bellwoods, this is shaping to be no mere buzz-off. Tensions are erupting, and the interested parties are out for more than electric circuits and wiring. A violent skirmish between the opinionations is at hand.

As the will-be combatants start taking positions with their respective bands, a handful among the Aisle 7 LARPers are uncertain which side to join. Attempts at their recruitment are soon made by the warring factions.

"Lend us thy swords, brethren!" says a voice in the Rig Mor throng. "Sisthren, will you consent to lending your mana against these oppressors?" is heard on the Nat Kon side.

Eventually, there is a fifty-fifty split after a couple of LARPers decide to remain neutral; specifically, the dwarf and the paladin. The sorceress joins Nat Kon, along with an archer, an Ewok, and a Quidditch beater. Rig Mor is joined by an assassin, a mage, a unicorn princess, and a Romulan. This is a bigger gathering of nerds than a D&D chatroom, thinks Bertram. Also, is that dwarf wearing fishnets?

The battle exceeds expectations. The sorceress gets the ball rolling with a paralyzing spell. It's a direct hit, and the mage trips on his robe and falls flat on his face. The neutral paladin assumes the role of peanut gallery and remarks, "Oh snap!" This is when the Quidditch beater makes her move. However, it backfires when the brush-end of her broomstick smacks a fellow Antifa Blackshirt across the face, slashing his cornea with the bristles. That makes two goals for Nat Kon, although one is an own goal. Rig Mor takes advantage of their adversaries' humiliating friendly fire to strike a blow at the sorceress, whom they consider the most dangerous threat based on how menacing she looks channeling energy with her scepter. The Romulan rises to the occasion, attempting to telepathically disarm the sorceress, but the sorceress pre-empts him with a counterspell. It's effective. The Romulan gets a migraine and is out for the count.

But then, a twist of fortune, as the unicorn princess proves a worthy substitute for the Romulan. It seems counterintuitive for a unicorn princess to have sided with Rig Mor, but it unravels that she is a staunch neoconservative and acolyte of Joel Osteen, whose face she brandishes on a pin attached to her rainbow suspenders. She strikes the ground with her hoof and charges like a bull at a matador. The result is a devastating double-blow for Nat Kon. The archer takes a hit in the pelvic region and an Abolish The Police petitioner loses her voice entirely in a single hysteric scream. But the unicorn princess does not walk away unscathed. The attack has cost her dearly, and she limps back to her line with a cracked horn. Seizing the opportunity, a nativist wielding a Confederate flag on the Rig Mor side yells, "Victory!" But his declaration is premature. At that precise moment, the Ewok barrels across the divide and takes the nativist down like a bowling pin. Meanwhile, the neutral dwarf has soiled his fishnets out of sheer excitement.

Another development is unfolding above the ground: the assassin has been stealthily crafting his surprise assault. His plan is to outflank Nat Kon and attack from behind enemy lines, taking advantage of the distraction caused by the events on the battlefield. His outflanking maneuver depends on him successfully scaling the racks separating the aisles, and in doing so unnoticed. But he has overestimated his acrobatic prowess. He only manages to reach the top of a rack stocked with Complicit in Whiteness Wong buzzbotz before he slips and ends up dangling helplessly above the crowd, wailing for an extraction squad. Making matters worse, he somehow manages to get his sword, which is strapped to his back, stuck in the ventilation duct directly above him, so that whenever he shimmies his hips in an effort to climb back down, the tip of the blade pricks his tailbone.

The RPG mode of combat suddenly gives way to battle royale as the screeching bulletin board of identity categories hollers, "Charge!" The other side reacts accordingly, and within seconds, the armies stampede at one another. The unfolding scene can only be described as macabre. The sorceress's scepter cracks upon contact with the young creationist's nose, which also cracks. The wounded unicorn princess has meanwhile plunged into rampage mode. In a remarkable display of soldierly grit, she dashes into the scrum and viciously slams the Ewok, sending him flying across the room. From her vantage point, it is like seeing a little person hurtling into an abyss: you're watching something small get smaller and smaller. "Oh snap!" says the paladin. The Romulan's splitting headache causes him to vomit; which ends up working in his team's favor, as it lays a deadly trap for the Antifa Blackshirt, who slips on the warm slop and lands hard on his left testicle. Somehow, the soiled dwarf now finds himself in the middle of the scrap. He has torn off his fishnets and is swinging them like a burlesque dancer's brassiere, in effect converting the soggy fabric into an excremental sling that befouls combatants on both sides. In a grisly act of battle lust, the archer is seen sodomizing the nativist with his own flag. All the while, the assassin remains stuck above the rack. Not only does his sword continue to poke him, but his vision is gone after shards of excrement have struck him square in the eyes.

The bloodbath persists for another eight minutes. By the end of it, the Romulan lies unconscious in a pool of throw-up; the Ewok complains about a broken rib; a bloodied unicorn princess is ramming the sorceress—whom she has overpowered—half to death with her broken horn; the screeching bulletin board pours salt on the ground like Scipio at Carthage; the Quidditch beater zooms madly around on her broom in a clear display of shellshock; the young creationist wails like a toddler, his pocket bible caked in snot and fragments of fecal matter; the mage cowers under his robe, licking salt off the floor to ease his nerves; the dwarf has removed his boot and has proceeded to use it as a latrine; the assassin has fainted atop the rack, his tailbone bloody and his face crusted with yellow bowel fluids; the archer sits ashamed in a corner, slapping himself as contrition for his violation of the nativist; and the nativist walks bowlegged off the battlefield, bent flagpole still jammed in his rear end. Fittingly, the paladin says, "Oh snap!" as if in recognition of the fact that no clear winner has emerged; and if one has, the victory is pyrrhic at best.

To a sane outside observer, the whole fracas might have looked like a simple case of rival gangs from the local asylum who had stopped taking their meds, made an escape, and ended up at Bertram's Emporium, proceeding to wail incantations at each other while swinging nerd paraphernalia around and defecating themselves as if the bath salts had just started kicking in. But that is not what it looks like to them. Because these combatants believe the truth of their madness: this description of events is how *they* lived it. You may think it is hyperbole, exaggeration, supernatural. But superstition is a prerequisite of the supernatural, which is a concept invented because nature and reality aren't good enough—not interesting enough, not deep enough, not holy enough—so it becomes necessary to invent enigmatic divinities and hallucinating prophets instead. And when those are not available in the present worldview, the superstitious find their solace in impossible spaghettis of conspiracy theorizing, in neologized fantasy labels designed to rename reality in order to subjugate it, in lizard pederasts, in a Luciferian Patriarchy, in a monolithic Police Force singularly made up of inhuman drones of destruction, in Lemuria, in Pizzagate, in homeopathy, in vitamin water, or in regression back to God, to Allah, and to Yahweh. And even though these objects of devotion only have reality in the identity-obsessed coconuts that wobble upon the shoulders of those who believe in them, that does not mean that the *consequences* of believing in them are any less real. And so, no matter how the spectacular brawl that has transpired at Bertram's on this fateful morning is described, the parties involved in it are all agents who acted on behalf of their beliefs, irrespective of whether reality confirms those beliefs on the basis of facts. The only fact here is that five young people are badly injured, a few are forever affected, and all the conscious ones are already posting about it in an effort to secure their narrative of the events. And somehow, in addition to all of that, Cornstalk and the Nesses have coordinated their arrivals precisely, and are marching through the Emporium's doors, beelining it straight toward Bertram and Joanna. And they look *pissed.*

9

It does not take long before the Nesses realize who Cornstalk is; that is, what the company he represents, is. The Nesses fix on him a basilisk-stare, eyes filled with dark red rage, like diva cups on heavy flow days.

"What in the Eff U Cee Kay is going on, Bertram?" says Ness 1. "And moreover, what in the cunting fuckballs is this Right Morals suit doing here? And, most importantly, *associate,* what in the shart-inhaling meth-koalas are *his* products doing on *your* shelves?"

"Behold," Cornstalk cuts in. "All along I have clandestinely diverted the contractual bonds that you, that is to say, the conglomerate whose standard you bear, underhandedly secured with this here purveyor of wares. Howbeit, be sure that this present scene of din, the which rivals the very slopes of Golgotha, was not a design of my own penumbral dealings with your commercial colleague, who is likewise and in simultaneity, my hitherto confidential collaborator. I hereby entreat the undersigned of our secret compact, *id est,* Mr. Bertram Cohn, to convey how our shared interests, along with the customers whom those interests safeguard, have come to such savage ends. Aha."

Before the undersigned Mr. Bertram Cohn has a chance to answer, Ness 2 chimes in.

"I see what this is. Rancid skid-marked laundry left out in the open air for all to sniff. You slid behind our backs, bucko, like an oiled gerbil, and made a deal with this fascist shit-petard whose merch is now shelved in the same shop as ours, threatening to outsell us. You've overplayed your hand, Cohn. You can bid *adieu* to this and every other future you planned on having, unless it's fluffing codpieces for shit-petard here."

"Not so agile," says Cornstalk. "Upon our rendezvous in closed quarters, wherein the aforementioned agreement was brokered, your man, that is to say, he whom you believed to be *your* man, revealed to me the circumstances of your so-named 'deal,' obtained under no other incentive than larcenous exploitation. Permit me to disabuse you, damsels, of your convictions concerning that deal so-named. In the accord *we* struck, in good faith perforce, a clause, whose importance will soon become apparent, was dutifully inserted, the which binds the outfit whom I represent to fully and exhaustively absorb the costs of Bertram's legal representation in, and moreover supply the legal team for, a defamation and libel lawsuit to be brought against National Konscience Viral Distributors, should you, that is to say, the company you represent, proceed with the spurious incriminations you have invoked to secure his cooperation. Aha."

The Nesses are fuming following Cornstalk's vainglorious gotcha moment. Their eyes are scarlet fury, the beady diva cups runneth over. And yet, the smoldering cauldron of hatred in their breasts erupts forth in the form of a paralyzing comeback. These are no amateur damsels that Cornstalk has just incensed. The Nesses play their hand, their minds are in tune as one, syntonized to a single frequency.

"Hey, Ness?"

"Yas, Ness?"

"What do you think about the optics on this tragic scuffle between innocent defenders of social justice and genocidal bigots of the Patriarchy?"

"Not cool beans, Ness. Not cool beans."

"Quite right, cool beans they are not. And who do you think the voices of the people will blame for instigating this exercise in toxic masculinity?"

"My educated guess, Nessy bae, would be the side motivated by systemic racism, sexism, homophobia, transphobia, lesbophobia, queerophobia, bisexophobia, asexophobia, disablism, anti-Hispanism, anti-Indigeneity, Romaniphobia, Islamophobia, and other historically less systemic forms of discrimination."

"Yes, the deck does seem stacked against that side. Because, and this is the thing, it is positively unconscionable for butchery of this kind to be initiated by victimized identities whose only cause is to speak truth to power and call for retributive equity. They are merely the voice of the silenced, called upon to redeem the downtrodden by being strong for the weak and brave for the meek, adulting on behalf of the infantilized, building community, and starting conversations. And then, there's the side across the aisle—that one, Aisle 7. What identities make up their ranks? White supremacists and homicidal policefolk. That limping nativist over there pretty well sums up their neo-Confederate agenda. And what identities make up our ranks? Martyrs of the intifada for inclusion, featuring a whimsical unicorn princess who broke her horn in a performative subversion of phallocentric symbols and, most empowering, a crossdressing little person who singlehandedly destabilized traditional latrinal practices."

"Ness, I can hardly think of more icky optics since former track-star-turned-trans-star-turned-traitor, Caitlyn Jenner, voted Republican. We're looking forward to the public burning of you two buckos once our narrative has made the rounds. Peace out, twats."

A promise of triumph washes over Bertram as he glances at Joanna. With a quick nod, he signals his satisfaction with how effectively the sabotage seems to have gone. Joanna, for her part, is astounded that this is Bertram's primary concern given the circumstances, which none of these assclowns has yet thought to do anything about. But she has exercised caution so far to avoid overstepping. And so, the ravaged battle scene remains undealt-with. The wounded still litter the shop floor when Cornstalk opens his mouth with a suggestion that threatens to derail the train wreck Bertram is hoping for.

"Aha, very bad. They are not bluffing, sirrah, you can be ascertained of that. It is imperative that we swiftly lick our abscesses and expedite new arrangements to prevent a total loss."

Cornstalk creates a mouth-whistle using his fingers and blows to call back the Nesses.

"Damsels, tarry a while and harken. The fork that splits our thoroughfare is such that one path leads to our separate destructions, the other, to our cooperative salvations. Yet I am confident that there is sufficient latitude betwixt us twain to settle upon mutually beneficial fiats for our respective corporate corpuses. What say you?"

The Nesses weigh the invitation.

"We're listening," says Ness 1.

"Let's talk terms," says Ness 2.

A horrified Bertram feels the blow of this wrench in his plans like a jackhammer to the balls. A moribund wheeze issues from the mound of injured. An enraged Joanna has had enough.

"Seriously, fellas, is any one of you the least bit *concerned* for these kids? Stop comparing clit sizes for a moment and look around you. If you genuinely care about these loyal likers of yours, you had better call an ambulance soon because that bowlcutted nerd over there is still lying unconscious in his own puke, that Antifa boy appears to have torn his nutsack, there's an archer cowering in the corner looking like he already has PTSD from his war crimes, and that shit-covered ninja requires immediate medical attention and a bath. Also, someone needs to report that depraved dwarf to the cops. He's been drinking his own piss out of that boot, and I'm pretty sure he molested himself with the other end of that flagpole."

But she might as well have chastised a bushel of wheat in an empty field. No recognition of her even having spoken is seemingly registered by her interlocutors. After what seems an unacceptably long lag, Bertram finally speaks up and sides with her.

"She's right, people. You—*we*—need to put our differences aside and get this freakshow taken care of."

But behind the façade is realpolitik calculation at play. At the very least, this momentary distraction buys him time to consider what to do about the motion that Cornstalk spewed out of the batshit blue to make a pact—or worse, a merger—between Rig Mor and Nat Kon. He cannot, he repeats, cannot let that happen.

10

It is, he repeats, it is happening. Fuck, fuck, a thousand times fuck.

Not two hours ago as the cock crows, these cretinous ambassadors of values were ready to go at each other's spinal cords with icepicks. Now, frolicking virtuously on their common grounds, they have successfully leveraged monetary incentives to convince the veterans of the Battle of Emporium Hill, as it has been christened on social media, to post a message of unity and defer blame over the rampage to enemies they can both agree on. The vets even volunteered hashtags in honor of the reconciliation: #defenestratetheelites, #wethenoble99%, and #pissbootchallenge. The fine-grained distinctions between The Deep State and The Establishment, Reptilians and Corporations, Globalists and Bourgeois Neoliberals, Educated Experts and Privileged, Jews and Zionists, have evaporated to give way to a single monolith, one which both camps are equally content to channel their resentment towards so that their grievances can coalesce into a single, pulsating orb of caffeinated truth-dropping and histrionic outrage.

By the time the ambulances leave the shop's premises, the hashtags are off to the races. Within minutes, they trend. Within an hour, they have viraled.

Defeated, Bertram mops the blood-and-feces-stained floors, gazing at Cornstalk and the Nesses glide across the parking lot, smug as conniving BFF tweens. And like conniving BFF tweens, the clique is enclouded by an air of villainous content at having rained a runny dump on their lessers, like a mist of unacknowledged flatulence in a vegan restaurant. Bertram, the lesser in question, finds no sympathy in Joanna, who has yet to show signs of lamenting the misfortunate Nat Kon and Rig Mor merger. Her head and heart are elsewhere;

namely, still furious at Bertram for his crass indifference to the juvenile warriors of the Battle of Emporium Hill.

"Did you hear me, Joanna? We are officially the indentured bitches of these ideological dementors. I'm out of ideas, save pilfering that ninja's sword to slit my wrists with. Aside from bending over and spreading our cheeks to hasten this anal gang bang, what are we supposed to do? Joanna?"

"I can't believe I went along with it. I'm ashamed, and it troubles me that you are not. They're *kids*, Bertram. And there was murder in their eyes. Over *what*? Over political catchphrases? Identity slogans? Some cheap catchall opinion? Over words, Bertram, that do not correspond to reality."

"Are you still hung up on that? Christ, Jo, don't you see that these kids are Maos and Mussolinis in miniature? They're not individuals, they're groupthink megaphones for agitprop. They're not people if their whole sense of personhood is reducible to the latest opinion to become clutch among the mob. Is that how 'clutch' is used? I've heard them say it before."

"It sounds like you are describing them as *condemned*, as if they're irredeemably doomed because of the opinions they identify with. That's rich, Bertram. Do I need to spell it out for you? Who you sound like right now? Like every self-glorifying, self-elective, self-blowing Abrahamic aberration that ever crowned itself the newest and truest truth of God and blanketed the rest with the filthy mantles of *goyim, pagans, heathens, dhimmi,* and *kafir*. That infantile division of the world is exactly the same as that which every populist politico and activistic firebrand prefers, all of them in stupid subservience to the mentally handicapped Manicheism of good-and-evil, heroes-and-villains, us-and-them, saved-and-damned. So save it, and damn you."

She's got me there, thinks Bertram. I'm a hypocrite. But as being confronted with your own bullshit sometimes goes, pride bests him. Consequently, the next words to leave Bertram's lips do not express an admission of error, but a doubling-down.

"If I wanted to be preached at, Jo, I would have gone to the Southern

Baptist Church. At least there I'd get chastised through song and rapture. And if airing dirty laundry is what we are going for here, then please accept my own jockstrap for you to chew on. All this time, you harp on about the 'principles of this store' and 'what it stands for,' like we're the fucking Bloomsbury Group. Let me tell you something. The Bloomsbury Group was a bunch of prissy pedants who thought they were being alarmist with their vanilla hedonism. They were the poor man's prelude of French existentialism except directed against Victorian stuffiness. And exactly like the French, they managed to be as delusional in their conviction that sipping brandy and being in throuples would set history aright. But unlike those self-important rebels of the coffee shop, this place does not stand for anything. It never has. It was never anything more than a lark: silliness and hilarity—sillarity—a place that doesn't take itself seriously so that its customers don't have to either. It may have gotten a chuckle out of the odd walk-in that managed to loosen their sensibilities over their cherished convictions, but it never stood or fell with that. Only now it has fallen, to the same forces whose eternal racket I had hoped to ignore out of relevance. And then you strut in pretending to be the guardian of the integrity of this store when, in reality, all you have managed so far is to get your knickers in a moralistic knot over the coddled ideologues and sanctimonious brats that define this depressing generation."

Joanna takes a breath and polishes her reply.

"I know you do not mean that, Bertram, because I know you are not such a brimstone pessimist yourself. Not that I'm letting this slide because of that. If there was anyone whom I considered above taking a jab at their opinions so damn personally, it was you. But clearly, I was wrong, you petulant satchel of dicks. And before you fire me for calling you that, let me spare you the trouble. I quit. Be so kind as to get yourself royally cornholed, you petulant satchel of dicks."

Joanna abandons the broom to gravity and storms through the shop doors, leaving them swinging behind her. Bertram drops to his knees theatrically, having known this would happen the moment he exhorted Joanna to chew on his jockstrap. But he allowed it to happen all the same, simply out of his petulant, dickful pride.

11

The last few weeks have aged Bertram. When you reach that point of inhaling cocaine with a straw whose official use is suctioning tapioca balls out of bubble tea, you only have two options. Either you admit you have a problem, or you put those skills to competitive use at a gathering of criminal defense lawyers. But Bertram didn't have any lawyer friends. In fact, his only real friend in recent memory had, last they spoke, insisted he get royally cornholed.

Bedraggled, unslept, and knackered by post-blow fatigue, Bertram sits behind the counter of the shop that had been muscled away from him in all but name by the newly minted Moral Konscience Cooperative. Shit, he forgot. They had taken the name, too. The sign above the shop formerly known as "Bertram's Emporium of Things People Say" now reads "Folks' Truth." This cruel reminder causes Bertram to once again regret not having pilfered that ninja's sword when he had the chance.

In the grainy depths of his visual field, a bright-colored patch grows larger, occupying more space in his vista, until the object is close, practically viral-shedding on Bertram. The patch speaks. "Excuse me, sir, ma'am, or plural-pronoun singular folk, I would like to pay for this truthbot."

Oh, right. Mor Kon Co-Op had also renamed the buzzbotz.

"$94.80," says Bertram, snapping out of his suicidal daydreams to take stock of the organism before him. The lines between identity types have consistently blurred since the merger. Most days, he is hardly sure what he is looking at anymore. He can make out certain characteristic traits here and there, picked out of motley mosaics of often contradictory ideas—not that the absence of logic ever stopped them. This particular organism—whether it is a sir, ma'am, or plural-pronoun singular folk is anybody's guess—wears Urkel-eyeglasses under a neon pink Friar Tuck haircut. The being carries a pocket watch, which it refers to as a "timepiece," snug in a front pocket jutting out of a mesh crop top. Through the crop top, a tattoo is visible just above the left breast: the Gadsden "Don't Tread on Me" coiled serpent. The creature also champions the shorts with knee-high socks style, while its footwear of choice—assuming that a *choice*, as opposed to plain ideological determinism, entered into it at all—is black leather boots with white laces, which is the signature Neo-Nazi skinhead combo. Whether or not the lifeform is aware of that thorny detail, or whether it would care either way, is unclear, seeing as it brandishes a hammer-and-sickle pin on its khaki shorts alongside a pentagram, an OBEY decal, a Sanskrit Om, the seal of the Knight's Templar, a daguerreotype of Grand Mufti Amin al-Husseini surrounded by a freedom watermelon, the Chinese pictograph for yak butter, the Proud Boys' rooster insignia, a trading card portraying the beloved Pokémon Squirtle, a Hufflepuff coat-of-arms, the Bitcoin logo, a caption that reads, "Beer is my spirit animal," and the supercharged Pride Flag whose inclusivity has been expanded to the infrared and ultraviolet edges of the spectrum. The being is also wearing a cape. The cape is admittedly pretty clutch.

The amalgam proceeds to speak. "I consensually *love* this series of Disney's Marvel's Transgender Spider-Person Political Agitation truthbotz."

Amalgam then taps the command button to share the wise words of the florid truthbot with Bertram. "My Spidey-Gaydar is tingling! Is there another brave superhero in this diversified neighborhood? Is it *you*? Let's celebrate our freedom with Colt ACRs and keep our friendly neighborhood *safe* from caravans of undocumented aliens and ethnic minorities. Up, up, and a-gay!"

Amalgam is obviously pleased with itself at having chosen this fabulous homunculus. A slurpy grin elongates itself across Amalgam's mug, which Bertram considers slapping clean off. But the species chimes in before that intention is acted on.

"It's such a powerful protest against the hegemonic Zio-power of the deep-immigrant Transarchy," it says. "It is *so* the conversation that I am all about in my ownmost truth."

Although it is the dozenth time Bertram has witnessed a customer reference some schizophrenic version or other of this newest iteration of The System, something breaks in him this time. In what he knows apodictically to be a futile gesture, he nevertheless launches into a preachy tirade against this tragic excuse of a person's view of selfhood.

"If your identity is a banner of protest, you are not 'being your ownmost you,'" he preaches. "On the contrary, you are defining yourself entirely based on what is outside of you. All this makes 'you' is a jittery loudspeaker of the soundbites of speech that *surround* you. In effect, that makes you the original buzzbot. It makes you Furby."

"Fur-who?" says Amalgam. "Oh, do you mean 'Turdy?' The TikTok page for Bowel Movement Positivity selfies? I love their new bravery post! 'Female-identifying folks go poopy too—deal with it!' They're the bravest."

Merciful Mohammed, thinks Bertram. This generation has finally come full circle. Joanna was right about the lack of subtlety of these young millennials and Gen-Zers—yes, the two overlap. Their total inability for nuance, their zealous dogmatism, and their self-serving delusions of moral purity have all conspired together to finally cause their parochial agendas to plummet to such septic degrees that they now celebrate the literal shit that comes out of them. Where is that ninja when you need him?

"I can't wait to show this to my klansfolksies!" says Amalgam once the transaction is complete. "Hope the rest of your day is full of penance in the eyes of Jesus Christ, our slaying Drag Queen and Savior. Add me on Turdy!"

Forget the ninja, Bertram thinks. I don't need him or his sword to expedite the deed. As soon as this shift is over, I'm smearing on blackface and punching a cop.

12

Weeks elapse but Bertram fails to see his plans for suicide-by-cop through. The closest he came was that one time he picked a fight with a mailbox. But that was only because he did a poor job measuring his acid intake earlier that evening and mistook the unsuspecting mailbox for the twisted dwarf from the Battle of Emporium Hill, who was intent on subjecting the enfeebled Bertram to all manner of scatological vulgarities. A shadow of his former self, Bertram wastes his days behind the counter like a ghost, cashing people out while numbly absorbing, customer by customer, identity by identity, the sweeping effects of the industry of culture that Mor Kon Co-Op has expertly insinuated itself into and come to dominate.

One purely topographical reform that the Cooperative insisted on was the shop's new playpen. "Conversation Land," as it is named, has been active for over ten days now. If the zealous who pilgrimage to Folks' Truth as if it were a garish Kaaba were not sufficiently self-infantilized, the playpen puts the nadir of toddlerhood within their reach. It works like this. The multifarious amalgams that have grown out of Mor Kon's petri dish of culture gather in the playpen, equipped with their truthbotz of choice. They activate the cheap tinker toys, and—you guessed it—"put them in conversation." When the botz say things they find agreeable, the amalgams slap their hands together like trained circus seals and emit shrill "Woohoos!" like Spring Breakers and collegiate feminists supporting their besties flashing their tits or speaking truth to power. When they find things the botz say disagreeable, they spark a racket to drown out the offending elocution, later crafting petitions with their Subversion Kitz to censure the reprimanded botz.

But today is different. The playpen is overcast by an unusual tension. The amalgams are not merely putting their truthbotz into conversations. Somebody has committed an unspeakable *faux pas* because the crowd is unsure if they should agree with or protest that last statement voiced by one of the botz. Some are even simultaneously jeering and clapping, like short-circuiting Jolly Chimps. And if not because Bertram happens to recognize the tone of the particular bot responsible for this mayhem, his soul would not have leapt back into his blinking corpse at that precise moment to reanimate him. That voice. It sends shivers down his spine; even though, once, it had brought him laughter.

"No means no!" resounds the tinny monotone. "Unless you are deconstructing the systemic oppression of yes/no binaries."

I thought I'd gotten rid of it, thinks Bertram.

And yet, there it is, aglow in all its hot pink glory—the Flitting Valley Girl buzzbot. It becomes gradually apparent why the amalgams are confounded over the buzzlinez intoned by this particular design. They don't get it, the joke. Because it calls for the impossible on their part: to see their own eye in their field of vision, or in this case, their own butts in the field of the joke.

"This is very problematic!" says one. "Rape is no laughing matter. It is the only lawful basis of abortion in the eyes of God, as long as the fetus is not past the sixth week."

Another says: "The tonal construction of this bot enforces the implicit bias that women are, like, totally not super smart and not as good as boys at, like, being CEOs and stuff, even though their rightful place is in the household, TBH."

Yet another rocks back and forth by the edge of the playpen, bellowing: "I don't want it! I don't want it! I don't want it!"

And for the first time in a long time, Bertram smiles.

As confusion makes its crude draft of a masterpiece, the Jolly Chimps lose their marbles left and right, and in short order, a truth-off gets underway. It is initiated by a Sarah Huckabee Bernie Sanders truthbot gone rogue. The bot pronounces something about deregulating the wicked billionaire corporations, at which point a White Trash Matters truthbot intercedes with a statement about how racial profiling by Antifa is making America worse again. One amalgam feels particularly triggered by this remark and hurls its Pedophile Pride truthbot at the White Trash Matters one, nicking it. The Flitting Valley Girl buzzbot enunciates, "This place is *so* random." Its statement enrages an amalgam holding a Darth Vader Ginsburg truthbot, which uses its lightsaber to maim the Valley Girl bot. But it barely manages to make a dent, and in the event, ends up chipping itself and shattering its lightsaber. The shoddy craftsmanship of the Mor Kon truthbotz is on full display.

Some amalgams have started to cry, their glittery eyeshadow smeared across their cheeks and running down their "Secession Now!" burqas. The one in the corner wails like a banshee: "I don't want it! I don't want it! I don't want it!" It is not long before truthbotz of all stripes lie strewn across the playpen: cracked, scratched, and even decapitated. The Valley Girl buzzbot is virtually unharmed. That is when Bertram realizes something odd peeking out from under the chipped coat of a Laissez-Faire Lenin truthbot, underneath the revolutionary's fragile mask of intelligentsia. It is a facial expression. But not just any expression. A *flatiron* expression.

"Kid," Bertram calls out to the one nearest the object. The amalgam looks up.

"'Kid' is actually *not* my preferred pronoun—"

"Shut the fuck up. Pass me that bot."

The kid, looking viscerally microaggressed by Bertram's curt dismissal of his pronoun preferences, hands over the bot and starts crying bloody victimhood, only to receive little by way of pity, since the others are too focused on their own embodied experiences of intersectional discomfort. Meanwhile, the layers peel off the bald Bolshevik's poorly crafted face with minimal effort. Bertram's suspicion is confirmed. It isn't Laissez-Faire Lenin at all. It's Laissez-Faire *Cornstalk*.

"Hey, you!" he calls to another amalgam.

"I don't actually go by 'you,' I go by—"

"Shove a sock in it, anusbrain. Get with the bot."

Visibly shocked, Anusbrain does as instructed. This bot, however, reveals not Cornstalk underneath the paint, but gradually discloses an intensely tense ponytail, crowning a facsimile of one of the Nesses.

Something tells Bertram that this is just the tip of the conspiratorial iceberg. Could it be that ... no, it didn't begin with ... did it? He rushes to the backroom, where the pre-merger Right Morals Viral Productions and National Konscience Viral Distributors stock is shelved. He reaches into a crate of Nat Kon's Gender-Fluid Fannys and lays out a handful of botz across his workshop counter, next to the coffee-stained monthly bulletin. Bertram slices through the thin casing with a boxcutter, tracing a ring around the shell, and effortlessly peels off the covering like a rind of grapefruit. The first bot is a Ness. He repeats the procedure for the second. Ness. He does it once more for the third. Cornstalk. Out of a sense of experimental due diligence, Bertram rummages through a crate of Rig Mor's Deplatformed Dons and subjects the carrot-colored botz to the same surgical procedure. The results are: Cornstalk. Ness. Ness. Cornstalk. Ness.

"Of course," says Bertram. "Of fucking course."

He rushes back into the shop. In the playpen, the amalgams are synced in a charade of crying, outraging, rallying, and staging insurrectionist gender-repeal parties. The more radical among them record grotesqueries for uploading to Turdy. One of them squats bareassed over a galosh, upping the ante of the #pissbootchallenge.

"The shop is closed, motherfuckers!" says Bertram. "Scram! Git! Little boy, stop sobbing like a tarty bitch and haul ass! And you three, pull up your chinos and stop filming each other's rectums."

But the amalgams just stare with doe-eyed confusion at the raging shopkeeper. Time to try another tactic: speaking to them in their own language, appealing to their own logic.

"You have exactly fifteen seconds to get out of this store before I start censoring my use of ethnic slurs."

That last entangled threat strikes the desired chord with the amalgams. Like a herd of startled cattle, they funnel out of the shop. In the sudden silence, guided by its voice, Bertram locates the Flitting Valley Girl buzzbot. Something tells him that it is here for a reason, as if it was meant to be found and provoke this very disruption. It *was*, he realizes, as soon as he notes the fresh etching on the back of the ironic hot pink case. He reads the engraving. And for the second time in a long time, Bertram smiles.

It reads, "If your opinions are too fragile to take a joke, they're not strong. They're laughable. –Joanna Bloom."

EPILOGUE

"A little to the left," said Bertram, even though spatial coordinates were relative in this space. The boutique was designed after the enclosed hexagonal chambers of Borges's Library of Babel. Positioning anything to one side or the other of anything else was a matter of where the racks stood *vis-à-vis* oneself because, in relation to the whole, they were simply beside each other. (For practical purposes, the entrance was used for reference, though there were partial racks above and around it, too.)

You are probably asking, "What is this 'boutique' you are referring to, throwing your reader into the epilogue *in medias finis?*"

Seeing as the story is now over, it would not be artless of me to just tell you in the service of wrapping things up. That said, I am obliged to disclaim that I am not a graceful wrapper. My gifts always look like the lovechild of Scotch Tape and Transgender Spider-Person if crystal meth had defined the gestational period. But enough about my weekend.

The boutique. Bertram opened it after the buyout by Mor Kon Co-Op. How did he manage to free himself from his contract with the sinister cooperative? With poetic justice, is how. Remember how he was muscled into that first agreement with the Nesses? Borrowing a tactic from their own playbook, Bertram found a way to hustle them through blackmail most foul. He threatened to disclose the truth about the truthbotz: that they were, well before the merger, thinly coated replicas of themselves. The way cult followers, both religious and political, are carbon copies of their dogmatic, firebrand, brain-wipe leaders. The way Ivy League undergraduates are mimicries of their dogmatizing, firebranding, brain-wiping miseducators. The way truthbotz are your favorite opinions embodied in miniature. You can draw your own conclusions about that realization. Bertram certainly did. His realization was that he could squeeze them for every penny they were prepared to offer for his silence, and subsequently fuck off, as far off and away from their narcissistic mitosis of ideology as possible, to start something new.

Bertram had this realization only after another, equally significant one. It would have been singularly pointless to "take on" the owners of the factories of culture. He did not fancy himself enough of a redeemer of the proletariat to embark on such revolutionary pipe dreams. Because as long as monolithic mobs—moboliths—of perpetual victims, whether "the proletariat," "the oppressed," "the *Volk*," "the ninety-nine percent," are sharted into existence out of the sphincter of resentment and sanctified as a group, the stupid Manicheism of good and evil, saved and damned, victim-makers and victim-mongers, dominates. As long as those homogenic moboliths are anointed in milquetoast elixir of "Truth," groupthink and the hivemind reign, and with them, the content-creators and allies of the group and the hive will continue to thrive, like sweat in asscracks in July.

Every minister of culture knows this. Hence the magnetism of that headless pumpkin of America First, who goads his mobolith with screeds that read like they were penned by a mentally handicapped orangutan. Did I say orangutan? Pardon me, I did not mean to insult the tender ape by comparing it to that malformed incarnation of ignorance and charisma—of ignorizz. Hence the cult of the collegium, headed by token EDI bureaucrats and whiney hackademics who hammer the postmodernist gospel of identity moboliths into their students' heads so that catechism flows from their mouths like rabies. Hence the journalists and anchors and authors and artists and actors and pundits and podcasters and public intellectuals and pseudo-intellectuals and private citizens who pliantly pry their anal cavities wide for the tornado of mobolithic pathos to spiral up through them like the torch of Lady Liberty, all the way up to the speech center, until the echolalia chambers are thundering in stereo. And all this adapted from the GOAT of mobolithic ventriloquism Himself, whose priestly and rabbinic and imamic vicars on earth cannot stop raving about His favorite group and its one true Truth ever since the Almighty lodged His immaculate fist inside them to tug at their vocal cords like holy sock puppets. But here I must apologize. I had said enough about my weekend.

So Bertram took the money and ran—a new shop, specifically. Bertram's Boutique of Thoughts People Had. The name was not as catchy as "Emporium of Things People Say," but catchy was no longer his aim. His aim was the opposite. The difficult to catch.

In the center of the hexagonal structure was an island sectioned in two, one half of which was the cash counter from which Bertram surveyed the human landscape. This was a more interesting undertaking here. Okay, maybe not more *interesting*. Even reality television shows about porkish housewives with the IQs of nail clippings could be described as "interesting." The process was more, let us say, rewarding. Because it was no longer about identifying types, but about observing the *shedding* of former types. The gradual transformations were notable in returning customers, especially once they gained enough confidence to make use of the other half of the island, on the flipside of the cash register, which provided a special service. No, not that kind of special service, you saucy satyrs.

The service consisted in facilitating no-holds-barred discussions between willing participants in an expressly unsafe space, as long as they supported their views with rational arguments and evidence, as opposed to ire-spewing sentimentalist claptrap or unverifiable "lived experience." It was refereed to flag and disqualify sappy sloganeering and moral bullying or in case things got out of hand; for instance, if they appealed to silencing tactics or seized hold of fishnets to sling fecal matter at their opponents. The dynamic of the discussion was structured by prompts that each side was given to defend. Then, the prompts switched, so that the side previously defending the prompt now had to oppose it. This service was voluntary, though incentives such as store credit and coupons were provided to entice participants. It had been her idea—she even mediated it herself—which is why the sign above it read, "Jo's Elenchus Arena." Originally, Bertram had offered to put her name on the shop's sign since she was a full partner. But Joanna had refused, rightly contending that it was already an uncatchy mouthful as it was. And besides, she said, when my name is on a sign, it will be for my own place. Fair enough, Bertram said, adding: "As long you give me the regular's discount." Fair enough, said Joanna.

The buzzbotz, too, had undergone changes, most notable of which was the fact that they were no longer called "buzzbotz." (Or "truthbotz.") Featuring cutting-edge electronics and software, as well as elegant hand-designed shells, the selection of boldbots paid tribute to bold thoughts by bold people, and included such favorites as Savant Socrates, Maverick Al-Ma'arri, Savage Spinoza, Hobbes of Hell, Hume of Doom, Walloping Wollstonecraft, Deadly Diderot, Kwintessential Kant, Mad Marx, Notorious Nietzsche, Dangerous Darwin, Candid Cady Stanton, Fiery Fred Douglass, Marshaling Thurgood, Strikeforce Solzhenitsyn, Jarring Joan Didion, and Killer Kołakowski. The design of the Hannah Arendt boldbot ("Ardent Arendt") was especially innovative. It was outfitted with animatronic circuitry that enabled it to raise a little cigarette to its mouth and puff it, emitting real smoke. It was pretty clutch. There were also contemporary series that featured figures as diverse as Neil deGrasse Tyson, Michel Houellebecq, Anna Politkovskaya, Slavoj Žižek, John McWhorter, Margeret MacMillan, Marina Abramović, Daniel Dennett, and celebrities like Bill Maher and Stephen Fry. Some had even agreed to lend their voices to the recordings.

But the biggest difference was the boldline-unlocking function. The boldbots included one or two snappy boldlines upon first activating them. Savant Socrates, for example, slinged the famous, "The unexamined life is not worth living." Purchase of a boldbot included a user manual in addition to an accompanying text by or related to the figure the boldbot represented. Dubbed "boldbooks," the texts included works like Plato's *Apologia*, which came with the Socrates bot. The *Supplément au voyage de Bougainville* came with the Diderot one. "An answer to the question: what is Enlightenment?" accompanied Kant's. You get the idea. The remaining boldlines were unlocked by inputting codes that appeared in random footnotes hidden within the accompanying boldbooks. This meant that users needed to *read* the boldbooks to discover the codes and unlock new boldlines. (This did not guarantee that they would do so: after all, they could merely skim the footnotes until finding the codes. But if they were going to put that much effort into it, they might as well read the damn thing.)

—

"Just a little more," Bertram went on. "That's good."

"The place is looking shipshape," said Joanna. "Though," she added, dialing it down to a whisper, "I'm not sure about the new hire."

She cautiously nodded at the employee whom Bertram was instructing to arrange the racks.

"Ariel?" said Bertram. "I give him a week before we both get sick of him. It feels like being around the rejected audition of a Monty Python tribute troupe."

"Heads up," said Joanna. "We've got a live one."

She gestured to the entrance. Once in a while, they got "live ones," which was their pet name for the sorts of reified cultural categories they used to get at the old place. More often than not, they were indeed looking for the old place. Under its new joint ownership, it bore the name "Emporium of Moral Konscience Truthbotz Inclusive to All Genders and Races (Mixed and Pure), Faith Crusaders, and Real Truth Seekers." Subtlety was not their forte.

Despite his underlying impulses, Bertram resisted the urge to redirect such patrons to Mor Kon's Emporium. He had learned, in no small part thanks to Joanna, to give them the benefit of the doubt. They were, most of them, kids; still just kids. And few things were more disheartening than seeing these kids so fixed and fixated in their convictions, entombed in things as fragile as opinions before any extracurricular life had been lived, before their personalities were rigidly carved out into camps by mobolithic ventriloquists. Bertram had learned to be more generous to them. And through this effort, he also came to learn that they were, most of them, willing to unhinge themselves from the regime of self-replicating automation that their fixed and fixated teachers and parents and friends and ministers and idols and podcasters and memes strived to keep them under. A well-placed insight could motivate them to kick aside their heaviest baggage of causes; and even to spit on it, through laughing teeth.

"Welcome," said Bertram to the live one. "How can I help you today?"

"Actually, my preferred pronoun is not the singular 'you' but the plural 'you.'"

"How about I just call you by your name?" said Bertram. "Mine is Bertram, like in the shop's sign. But you can call me Bert, like the closeted Sesame Street character."

Live One seemed to appreciate the relatable reference. "My name is Charlee."

"So it is a 'my,' not an 'our'? As in, singular?"

"Sometimes it's singular, sometimes it's plural. They're all cisheteropatriarchal constructs anyway. This is how we destabilize them."

"Truth be told, Charlee, I don't feel like destabilizing anything before I've had my coffee. Do you know that feeling?"

"In that case," said Charlee, "please refer to me by the singular 'you.' And I do know that feeling. It is especially tough to overthrow the Patriarchy after a two-night bender involving bubble tea straws and copious amounts of blow."

Bertram flashed a smile.

"Charlee, do you know who else enjoyed copious amounts of blow? I have his boldbot right here, let me show you. Fantastic Mr. Freud. He is part of our Masters of Suspicion collection. He was deeply influenced by another bot in that series, Notorious Nietzsche, who also dabbled in self-medicating as a way to deal with his crippling health conditions. He was a real trooper, and had a few choice words about religion and herd mentality. You have undoubtedly heard of Marx, but have you *read* him? His critiques of ideology are poignant, even if he was ultimately wrong about practically everything. But the man's ideas shaped world history fundamentally, like few before have. The best thing about these boldbots? You don't put them "in conversation." These are programmed to be put into *dialogue*. In fact, one of our topsellers wrote only in dialogue form: Powerhouse Plato. Believe it or not, he proposed a communistic vision millennia before Marx, even though it was a pretty far-out version. Another far-out thing him and his entourage engaged in were these parties where they would drink urn after urn of wine while debating philosophy and engaging in wild orgies with their young cupbearers. They understood a thing or two about eroticism, the Ancient Greeks. Just make sure not to try any of it at home. You'll get arrested faster than you can say 'catamite.'"

"Catamite?" said Charlee.

"Never mind. Any of these calling your name?"

"Do you have any BIPOCs? I identify as BIPOC. Black, Indigenous, or Person of Color. I identify as one, some, or all of the above depending on the lunar phase at the time of identification."

"I'm not sure how to respond to that," said Bertram. "But bear with me, I will try my best. Let me see, how about this one? I think you may dig it, John McWhoopass. It is based on one of the most prescient and polished voices on race relations in America in recent decades."

Charlee's ears pricked up at that pitch. Bertram took down the John McWhoopass boldbot and displayed it on his open palm.

"See?" said Charlee, admiring the paint job on the cacao-tinted bot. "He too identifies as BIPOC."

Unsure how to respond to that, Bertram activated the bot.

"Victimology is not about change; it is all about nothing but itself," said the sultry voice on the recording.

"I do not like things that are not for change," said Charlee. "This 'Victimology' sounds very unprogressive. I identify with this McWhoopass."

Bertram grinned. "Tell you what," he said. "Pick another boldbot, anyone you want, and I will throw in McWhoopass for free. Two for the price of one, just for you. BIPOC Special."

Charlee's eyes lit up at the offer. If there was one thing we could all still agree upon in this divisive world, it was appreciating a good bargain.

"Who's that one over there? Strikeforce Sol-zhe-nit-syn?"

"You have a good eye, Charlee," said Bertram. "This is a solid combo."

He whistled to the new hire and gave him his instructions.

"Show Charlee here how the boldbots work."

Making his way across the shop, Ariel thought it would be uproarious to break into an imitation of the Ministry of Silly Walks.

Bertram massaged his temples upon witnessing the hackneyed stunt. It wasn't particularly silly.

PLEASE USE OTHER DOOR

2:32 PM

Some parents teach their kids that if they don't have anything nice to say, they shouldn't say anything at all. It's like my mom used to tell me, "I know you have money saved up from your paper route, Joanna, and Mommy needs her happy juice. But Daddy drank it all and blew his paycheck earlier this week. Sometimes, the best gift you can receive is the gift of giving. Happy ninth birthday."

I say fuck that noise. I had to pull myself up by my ovaries and tell my deadbeat bitch of a cunt mother where to shove my paper route. I speak my mind and whoever doesn't like it can grow the fuck up and stop being such a mewling shriveled nutsack.

Speaking of things that house genitals, this is the section where we keep the briefs.

Welcome back to the tour.

BITE-SIZED BITS: BAWLUME 2

A SEQUEL? JUST A SECOND

"Give it to me straight, Doc. Have I got the clap?" "The clap?" "It's slang for gonorrhea." "My dear boy," said the doctor. "You've received a round of applause."

Judas Priest, KISS, Barenaked Ladies, Beastie Boys, and Black Sabbath once formed a supergroup. They were called Priests Kissing Barenaked Boys on the Sabbath.

It is one thing to be a person who can hardly put up with things, it is another to be putting hard things up into your person.

The Son of God was a fisher of men, but a son of cod is a manner of fish.

He told a semitonal dad joke. It landed flat.

A man is being charged for hurling a breaded poultry tender at an underground shaft worker. He is accused of chicken-fingering a miner.

"Take my word for it." "What's *your* word for 'it'?"

There are two good things a man can stand to lose in life: his pride and his virginity. Some lose both in the same twelve seconds.

You can take the pun out of the sex joke, but you can't take the sex joke out of the poon.

Don't throw out the baby with the bathwater. Unless the baby is riddled with infectious disease.

A semitonal dad joke hopped onto its donkey. It landed flat on its ass.

If you split agricultural laborers in half, you get peas and ants. Which means peasants can just as quickly have a picnic as ruin it, too.

It takes two to tango, but only one to go tan.

A guest must have been enjoying the cheese too close to the bar. There was a curd in the punchbowl.

Two heads are better than one. Unless both times you picked tails.

A headline reported on the CEO of an electronics chain purchasing a fair-haired woman's tasteless cereal company, only to find that it was bankrupt. It read, "Blonde broad's bland bran brand bought by Best Buy boss but bust."

It is one thing to taint a fellow's name and be his downfall, it is another to name your fellow and fall down on your taint.

"To err is human; to forgive, divine." —Alexander Pope. "This Church's pederasty and graft are human errors. God is divine. Do the math." —Pope Alexander.

The Who, Duke Ellington, Bananarama, Cream, and Humble Pie once formed a supergroup. It was called Who Duked in the Banana Cream Pie?

A semitonal dad joke arrived at its London apartment. It landed flat in its flat.

Jesus said, "It is easier for a camel to go through the eye of a needle, than for a rich man to enter into the kingdom of God." Evidently, he never saw how easily a rich man can purchase a camel, liquify it, and drip the contents through a needle's eye.

He would fall asleep and lose his limbs. He had narcoleprosy.

A guest from a minority Iranian ethnicity must have been enjoying himself too close to the bar. There was a Kurd in the punchbowl.

While collectively applauding the performance, the ladies started menstruating and tried to conceal it. It was a standing ovation ovulation obfuscation.

Descartes declared, "I think, therefore I am." Shakespeare stressed, "I **think**, there**fore**: iambs."

Justice is just ice, which makes revenge a dish literally best served cold.

A headline reported on a possible connection between Southeast Asian critters and a Tiki cocktail hour, you dig? It read, "Thai mites might tie to Mai Tai time, a'ight?"

Take my advice because I don't want it anymore.

The biblical commandment to be fruitful and multiply has been sorely misunderstood. All God wanted was for us to gorge on mangoes and practice arithmetic.

Idea for drinking game: acquire venison, liquify it as rich men do camels, pour into highball, enjoy on ice.

You can take the bass out of the sea, but you can't take the C out of the bass. (If you don't get it, don't fret.)

They say brevity is the soul of wit. The wittiest person is therefore nothing but brief. The wittiest person is therefore underwear. Witty tighties, to be exact.

The man said he badly needed a stiff one, so I recommended Viagra.

It is one thing to put up photos spanking a child by the banks of the Volga, it is another to divulge photos of a child to put in the spank bank.

There must have been more than two things too close to the bar that night. There was a third in the punchbowl.

** Rim shots all around, on me. **

3:04 PM

There is no God and we are alone in this icy universe, biding our time until our withering bodies disembowel themselves and consciousness is extinguished for eternity.

But not all things are rainbows and butterflies. Life is just as likely to be butterfly shit and rainbow piss. And lucky for you coprophiles, we have devoted a special section to how to wade through the waste like fucking champs.

Take it from me. I used to be a helpless alcoholic. Now I'm a helpful one. After all, I'm helping you sorry lot. Now enjoy the goods while I go fetch my happy juice.

MISS GAYÏD'S SIX STEPS TO SUCKSESS

Sucksess is fugacious commodity in after-modern globe we inhabitate. Unsighted chance impedes even most athletic exertions at Sucksess. But with miniscule aid from Miss Gayïd, you as well can to eschew terrible potencies that conspire against your obtainments. Solely abide by these six rudimentary steps and you will convert into voluminous Sucksess!

STEP 1: PROVOKE UPLOADABLE SOCIAL OUTRAGE.

As Madison Avenue stout feline once exclaimed, there is nothing such as bad publicity. And that sack of douche was correct. There are multiple reliable fashions to provoke uploadable social outrage.

Miss Gayïd's top selection is for publicly castigating preferences of pronoun on university campus in front of indignated activists. These righteous commoners will defiantly position cellular mobile cameras at you, meanwhile condemning with many rackets and chants of "Shame!" Once time that content is onto TubeYou—hello illustrious new career! (Not to mention, hefty new paycheck, made out to J. Sonpeter.)

Congratulatings, you have converted into intellectual celebrity Sucksess. Do not neglect to appreciate your sponsors. Thanks you, indignated activists!

STEP 2: DO NOT POSSESS PEN PAL WHOM WITH YOU EXCHANGED CASUAL HOMOPHOBIC SLUR IN 1998.

You probably reminisce of time when you wrote to Dikambe in Angola about how seventh birthday party it was "very swell and gay." If this memory instigates horrors and bumps of goose in you, your fear is validated. It is not sufficient just to accomplish Sucksess in this canine-ingest-canine globe. You must to retain it as well.

To obtain such, it is predominant to avoid having written homophobic slurs to correspondent or confidant in years previous. Also, it is predominant to avoid having selected black Power Ranger as most preferred for Halloween costume if your exodermis is brighter than terracotta shade and you do not possess helmet covering your face.

STEP 3: DO NOT TO BE WHITE MALE.

Believe or no, there was time when being White Male did not make you destination of aggregated raging and contempt—indeed, it was asset even. However, being White Male today is handicap. Thanks yet to these art-of-state techniques, your White Maleness can be thing of past and your future can to be glorious Sucksess!

Technique first: identify as one genderqueer. You may not be capacious to expunge your delinquent Whiteness, but contentedly, your Maleness can to be improved. Most effectual fashion to identify as one genderqueer is to exclaim that you identify as one genderqueer. In Sucksess vernacular, this is named "outing yourself." Outing yourself should be performed resolutely and on every occasion that summons, like job interview, on In Linked profile, in societal congregation, during diplomatic mission, before procuring eulogy, while observing moment of silence, as you partake in three-leg race, or when positioning drive-thru order. It is as well particularly utile for rejecting advances of clerics.

But if despite great self-outing exertions, you remain too much "cis" to identify as one genderqueer—if, for example, you cannot to halt yourself from putting on jersey of baseball while consuming Miller's Lite—do not to despair. You may not be capable for vanishing toxic Maleness you harbor, but you can to employ technique second for to do something about supreme Whiteness. Among marvelous technologic progressions, *tanning bed* is most expedient mechanism for you to bronze away pesky Whiteness. Few sessions in tanning bed and even Irishes can to appear in more acceptable skin pigment.

STEP 4: BE DISENFRANCHISED MINORITY.

Unakin to Step 3, this step is hoped for more inclusive audience because it has application to White Females; whom which, according to Sucksess charts, rank under Terracotta Males but above of Terracotta Females.

Please to recall, as with TubeYou and tanning beds, modern technology is your comrade. DNA test kits can to be requested for your home and dispatched to laboratory in few days, and results may congenially amaze you! Do you possess insufficient racial purity for diversity-hire quota at roadside Arby's you solicited for? Do not to weep for me Argentina, because you may to discover you are 20% Argentinian. (In Sucksess vernacular, this is named "Latinx.") Do you aspire to snag hirement at cigar store? Your DNA may to include 6% Cherokee requisite to astound your employer.

Adding, your newly uncovered disenfranchised minority is assertable to attract many comrade allies into your orbit. As corporational large toupees know, what is Sucksess if without persons sucking up to your cess?

STEP 5: MANUFACTURE COMMUNITY.

There is in present no more predominant cause to exclaim devotion for than "manufacturing community." But possess caution. It is of cruciality that you manufacture community with mind-likened comrades. Therefore, acquire lessons from religions of great Sucksess.

Who does not make subscription to Truth of your community is named one antagonist. In exclamation of Lord Jesus the Christ, "He that is not with me is against me" (Matthew 12:30). If antagonist originates threat to Truth of your community, procure creative solutions, like illustrious Mohammedan recitation: "Those who blasphemed against Our revelations—We shall scorch at a Fire. Whenever their skins are charred, We replace them with new skins, so that they taste the torment. God is Almighty, All-Wise" (Qur'an 4:55). In Suckess vernacular, this is deadnamed "destructing career through storm of Twitter." Online opinion is Almighty, All-Wise.

STEP 6: BE ONE REVOLUTIONARY.

Being one revolutionary is expedient ticket to Sucksess. It supplies impeccable moral credentials, bold eyeglasses for statement of penetrative intellect, and adding, it converts you into total bad bottom. Because no one can to resist valiant spokesperson of trodden-down. Just make witness of moist infatuation aroused by Lord Jesus the Christ!

First requisite to become one revolutionary is middling-class background. If you emerge lower on social stratosphere, you may not to have access to tools for combatting System, such as degree of college. (Do not to take Step 4 too far away. If you are too much disenfranchised minority that you emerge poor, your crime-infestated neighboring hood may will not acquire benefit from revolutionary objective of abolishing police.)

Once you have emerged in middling-class habitat, produce societal media accountings for to upset System from inside. There is nothing System unenjoys more than viral "truth-explosives" that repel corporational billionaires at Bookface and X.

But do not limit your message to cybering space. Astound your peers at coffee shop by putting on graphical tee procured on Amazon market which makes warning "Revolution will not to be televised." This graphical tee is ascertained to make your comrades moist.

FELICITATIONS!

You now possess utensils for converting to Sucksess! Time to proceed out there and display to globe of what you are composed.

3:43 PM

You know kids. Always horsing around, scraping their knees, smearing feces on each other, eating those feces and contracting violent cases of dysentery, expelling even runnier feces suffused with blood, growing increasingly gaunt and pallid from extreme fluid-loss, and finally expiring in a puddle of their own filth. You know. Kids.

Which is why we aim to stay one step ahead of trends in juvenilia. By the time Tamagotchis make a comeback—mark my words, they will: I have a sixth sense for these things—we will be ready.

Don't believe me? Be so kind as to royally cornhole yourself, you bulbous anal abscess. Here is incontrovertible proof that we are hip with the youth.

MEMEOGRAPHIES

A consortium of investigative journalists tracked down iconic memes, both current and forgotten by 2017. These are the stories of those viral behemoths, straight from the sources' mouths.

HIPSTER BARISTA

I won't never forget that fateful day. So, I's in the back, the usual, emptyin' the grease trap and whatnot. All a sudden, Uncle Sal calls, the big boss man.

He says, "Hey Pauli!"

I says, "I'm busy with the grease trap, Sal!"

He says, "Take off the hairnet. You're going to be in a photoshoot."

Uncle Sal, he proceeds to explain I got the vigor of youth. I'm a photogenie, he says. Then he says I best cover my neck tattoo on account of it ain't salutary for business. So I takes this long black rag, right, and wrap it around like 'em turbans what the Hindoos is wearin', except on my neck on account of that's where the ink is. Now this photographer, she represents a small outfit, some wine and dine periodical. Lo and behold about a month later, my cousin Frankie sends me this link, says it's hot, he says. I click it, and lo and behold, there I am, Ginger Pauli, lookin' fresh in my frames, with some quote attributed to me about a spicy pumpkin or somethin'.

But hey, I don't mind. As Ginger Pauli says, "If you'se makin' meat sauce, you don't install no cheap linoleum."

HIDE THE PAIN HAROLD

To many, I am Harold, which is *not* my Christian name. Yet to others, I am merely "smiling old man meme."

This simple description, erasure of my identity, is made worse by its gratuitous assumptions about my age. I am only thirty-two. I suffer from a rare condition that causes albinism of the hair, wrinkling of the skin, and incontinence of the bowels. The "smile" is an involuntary mandible contraction: a side-effect of my enfeebling medication. But those cavalier adolescents whose cybernetic amusement is pilfered at my expense—what would they know of that? To them, I am no more than a visual punchline, a pixelated image fit for lampooning, behind which neither heart nor feelings are presumed to dwell.

"Hide the Pain Harold," I have been branded by cruel circumstance. Well, I herald you this: the pain hides no more. Now you see me. Beneath the smiling old man is a bruised and melancholy soul.

CARDBOARD SIGN GUY

What people don't realize is that the sunglasses are because I'm visually impaired. In fact, my early career failed to launch because the signs were all in braille.

Then came Lucinda, my agent. She spotted potential in me, or at any rate, in my *medium* of messaging, since the messages themselves she couldn't decipher. That's when people started noticing. I would dictate and Lucinda would write the signs. She insisted on keeping the grassroots aesthetic, which had the added advantage of minimizing expenses since production costs would be devoted solely to markers, cardboard, and a budget photographer. The only other cost was creativity. At first.

As the star of my celebrity rose, pressure mounted to come up with more and more slogans. Memedom is not all it's cut out to be. Work was all-consuming. My wife left and took the kids, leaving behind only cardboard cut-outs of them. I would caress their thin, corrugated bodies at night, until my dog viciously mutilated them and urinated on the mangled remains. I became addicted to markers, enslaved to the toxic fumes of jet-black ink. Meanwhile, the industry kept on grinding me down.

I've never confessed this to anyone, but I've already composed my final sign; my send-off, written in the same style of that first attempt, long before the meme-madness.

It reads: ⠠⠛⠕⠕⠙⠃⠽⠑ ⠉⠗⠥⠑⠇ ⠺⠕⠗⠇⠙.

GRUMPY CAT

Rivkat! Be a kitten and fetch me a saucer of milk! The lactose-free kind, otherwise I'll be sitting *shivah* in the litterbox for the death of my colon.

Whoa, are you writing this down? God forbid you give an aging tom a heads-up. I'm here grooming my *kishkes* and you're turning it into erotica!

How'd I make the Big Time, you ask? Truth is, "Grumpy" is a misnomer. Pestered? Sure. Miffed? Absolutely. Vexatiously irked? Indubitably. But I'm no grump. As a matter of fact, back in Beit Meow High School I was voted most likely to enjoy a career in impromptu carpet-vomiting; which, as any feline enthusiast knows, is a path intended for *naughty* cats, or at most, *insouciant* ones, but not grumpy.

Lady Fortune, however, had other plans. She's slippery like that. You let your paws down for one moment, the next some camera-wielding *putz* happens to be in the right place at the right time, and your fate gets sealed like a can of sweet, sweet tuna.

Sure, I enjoyed the notoriety. I even earned the respect of a few street strays. But at what price? Don't answer that, it's a rhetorical question. It used to be, there was more than one way to meme a cat. But no sooner than *this* cat was made into a meme—into a one-dimensional, one-trick tabby—the meme became the cat, and the cat became grumpy indeed.

Rivkat! Who's a four-legged friend gotta *shtup* around here to get a *farshtunken* saucer of milk!

See what I mean?

THE MOST INTERESTING MAN IN THE WORLD

I don't always talk about my personal life, but when I do, I wear women's lingerie.

You see, I don't always expect people to grasp the challenging depths of the most interesting man in the world, but when I do, I hope they consider that the most interesting man in the world might also be the most—damaged.

It may seem like I'm always brimming with confidence, but when I'm not, that's my authentic self breaching through the façade of personhood in which internet fame has encased me, the way a slick bottle of Dos Equis™ encases its crisp, cool lager within: bounded by an assertive exterior that, upon closer examination, is fragile as glass.

I don't always trust a beloved meme to be treated as a human being subject to the trials and tribulations of this vale of tears, but when I do, I only ask that you remember: there is a *me* in "meme."

In fact, there are *dos*.

4:22 PM

This may come as a surprise, but I am no poetess. The only resemblance between me and Sappho is that I also prefer the odd helping of taco juice to a faceful of eggplant milk. Besides, I can't rhyme for shit, let alone time a hit to coincide with the meter like a wife to her beater.

Well fuck. And here I thought I was only good at inhaling lines; turns out I can drop them too, the way a wife drops her beater when she's scrambling eggs. You thought I meant a different kind of beater?

Maestro, activate the bot.

WHERE THOUGHTS AND PRAYERS GO TO DIE

Midway through life I found a place
Where thoughts and prayers go to die,
And good intentions leave no trace.
Its tour guide is a rancid guy,
Who bellows like a manic nun
And smells like week-old cabbage pie
That has been sitting in the sun.
The rancid guide, he takes my hand,
Says, "Let me show you how it's run."
The circle first is rather bland,
It's just the prayers for dads and moms
With shitty children they can't stand.
With circle two I have no qualms,
It's futile prayers for high school gals
Who got knocked up on senior proms.
"To circle three, my friends and pals!"
Where rot the prayers against disease
Alongside their own rationales.
The circle fourth, it guarantees
That written prayers create no waste
Save breath and ink and time and trees.
"To circle five we must make haste!"
So not to miss the praying-depraved:

The groveling God-bedeviled caste.
	Their thoughts and prayers are well-behaved,
Just like the altar boys they fix.
"Forgive me Lord, I have but craved!"
	The thoughts and prayers and heartfelt pics
Well-wished to those mowed down in schools
To circle six sink down like bricks.
	The mosque and church and temple fools
To sphere the seventh sacrifice
Their kneeling pleas to vengeful ghouls.
	And thus they pray away their vice,
With wink in eye to lackey Lords,
Who love a sin bought at fair price.
	"Now circle eight we head towards!"
Where weepy politicians' speech
Strikes no more sentimental chords.
	Instead, for being such a leech
That mewls in the public ear
It should be booted in the geech!
	Yet punishment ain't meted here:
You cannot hurt what ain't alive,
Not even down in this ninth sphere,
	Where thoughts and prayers are thought to thrive
Like sweat in asscracks in July.
But prayers and thoughts do not arrive:
	They're neither sent, nor go to die.

4:49 PM

It is my firm belief that our culture does not give performers of make-believe the veneration they are due.

Can you fathom the level of bodily self-awareness needed to become an expert on contemporary geopolitics and diplomacy? Or the hours of makeup until you can codify moral principles into sociolegal norms? What about the mastery of mnemonic techniques required to grasp the psychophysical benefits of inserting jade obelisks up your rectum?

They do. And it is about time they were given a platform to drop the nuggets of wisdom they are privy to on us sub-thespian dimwits, the way a privy is privy to the dropping of nuggets from privates in private.

So make like a privy and pipe down, fucktarts. The grownups are speaking. Prepare to be humbled.

INSIDE THE HACTORS STUDIO

"Hello, and welcome to another edition of *Inside the Hactors Studio.* As always, I'm your host, Anus Panderson. I'm joined today by three luminaries of the silver screed. My first guest is Leopoldo DiCrankio. Drawing on his lifelong background in acting, improv, interpretive dance, and charades, Leo serves as U.N. environmental ambassador and honorary expert in multilateral diplomacy. Over the past ten days, he flew to fourteen countries, drove to over thirty receptions and fundraisers, and delivered over fifty transatlantic sermons on the urgency of climate change, leaving his indelible footprint in the struggle against our dying planet. Welcome, Leo."

LEO: Thank you, Anus.

"My second guest's storied career includes such passion plays as *That's Rich: Dumping on the Wealthy* and *Sophie's Gender Choice.* She is the recipient of the Most Virtuous Pontification Hacademy Award for her speech, *Righteous Indignation on Behalf of the Cognitively Divergent.* Please welcome Myrtle Strap."

MYRTLE: I would like to take this opportunity to reflect on those who are traditionally deprived of the means of joining this programming today: communities affected by the lack of access to cable television, which survive on as low as one streaming service for their content. Shame be on us all.

"Thank you for that powerful call for equity, Myrtle. Finally, we are blessed to be joined by the first member of Hollywoke to undergo ethnicity reassignment surgery, Bruce Lee Jender. Bruce is an icon of the Trans-Asian community, as well as the Nobel Prize awardee for Bravest Procaryotic Organism. It's an honor to have you with us."

BRUCE: Ni hao, Anus.

"Let's start with you, Bruce. I understand you took some heat in your native Hong Kong for siding with the anti-transethnic policies of the Jinping administration. Yet you yourself are a brave member of the transethnic community. How do you reconcile your bravery with your ideology?"

BRUCE: There is an ancient Confucian saying: *"Let he who rustles the feathers of the rooster and pinches the buttock of the hen lose his own cock and have not eggs again."* If you and your viewers do not understand, that is because you have not lived my Oriental truth.

"I am humbled at being called out on my ignorance, Bruce, and will make a better effort to learn about this important conversation. On to you, Myrtle. Tell the audience about the new project you are directing."

MYRTLE: The film is titled *Blind Justice*. It is about the struggles of an optically-shamed lesbian suffering from ADHD who has been uprooted from her native Saudi Arabia and forced to immigrate to California, where she faces the systemic discrimination of Berkeley University. The film is a protest against the oppressive casting practices of the industry, which historically has hired only optically conformant folk for the roles of the optically shamed, such as Al Pacino in *Scent of a Ciswoman*. My film is boldly trailblazing the path forward, overturning the hegemonic status quo by casting a real blind BIPOC genderqueer in the role of blind BIPOC genderqueer.

"I see, so she's playing herself. I was not aware it was a documentary."

MYRTLE: It is not a documentary, Anus, and your assumption is both shocking, problematic, discriminatory, and genocidal. I am obliged—nay, obliged—to drop this truth-bomb on your implicit prejudice that the role of blind BIPOC genderqueer should be acted by someone who is not a member of the blind BIPOC genderqueer community. It is both disablist, racist, homophobic, and fascist. Since the dawn of unicellular life, elites in positions of power in the film industrial complex have normalized the othering bias that acting consists in assimilating the experiences of others by empathetically identifying with them to give expression to another's world. My film is dedicated to dismantling that history of emotional appropriation and biographical colonialism.

"I am humbled at being called out on my ignorance, Myrtle, and will make a better effort to learn about this important conversation. Leo, the press is just *adorbing* your new campaign for the Seychelles. Can you tell us about it?"

LEO: As Climactic Counselor for Amnesty International, over the past year, I have undertaken no less than twenty-nine diplomatic missions to the imperiled Seychelles islands, departing from over thirteen destinations, some as far as eleven time-zones away with four layovers. I have personally hosted seven *Diamond Galas*, five *Fêtes d'Or*, three *Learjet Socials*, and two *Junipero Jamborees*—one of which took place in Macau, while the other was two refueling stops away, in San Francisco. The funds raised through these efforts have all gone toward the Save the Seychelles campaign, after expenses.

BRUCE: I attended one of the *Junipero Jamborees* in Macau, Leopoldo, and I speak for all members of the Trans-Asian community when I say that the lack of representation of the Manchurian-presenting polysapient community of the People's Republic of China was appalling and fascist.

LEO: I am humbled at being called out on my ignorance and will make a better effort to learn about this important conversation.

MYRTLE: Bruce drops an important truth-bomb. You would not understand this, Anus, since you are optically shamed by your privilege. But like Macau, Hollywoke too is plagued—nay, plagued—by its lack of representation of folk in the community of Trans-Asian Manchurian-presenting polysapiens of the Neo-Maoist persuasion (TAMPPoNMaP). Why just in the previous Hacademy Awards ceremony, which Leo flew from Novosibirsk to host before flying back to Swaziland, a mere three TAMPPoNMaP feature films were nominated, with only two winning in their respective categories. Even more postcolonial was the fact that just five TAMPPoNMaP actors were nominated, and of those, only three won—all in *supporting* roles, in other words, in traditionally subjugated roles.

"Myrtle, you anticipate my next question while giving me a lot to be humbled about. What, if anything, is to be done about the toxic culture that suffuses the world of Hollywoke celebrity? When will nonparaplegic white males cease appropriating the roles of the motor functionally-divergent, like Daniel Day-Lewis in *My Left Foot*? When will merely bisexual women stop stealing the limelight from fully gay and even pancurious women?"

MYRTLE: Chances are body-shaming, Anus, as the hegemony of your people is both at its most disablist, racist, homophobic, and fascist on record. Underrepresented Hollywoke actors are being drawn and quartered daily by movie producer elites, when not forced to star in their own Netflix originals.

LEO: Not to mention that those producers get paid to sign contracts on paper, which is made from tree pulp. Those corporate fat cats deforest the Amazons while counting their money, which is also made from paper, meaning that they fund deforestation with the product of that deforestation. In fact, I am starring in a movie to raise awareness about it called *Defenestrate the Deforesters.* The film will be set in nine of the world's most secluded natural forests, to which we will be airlifting real lumber mills in order to showcase the kind of destruction these producers wreak on the environment.

MYRTLE: Leopoldo, I would like to be an ally of this project as its casting director. To raise awareness about the Amazons, it is imperative that you hire indigenous Amazonians to star in the roles of indigenous Amazonians. Privileged for you, my agent has exclusive access to isolated tribes of Brazil that can only be reached by helicopters departing from São Paulo after you have flown there from Seattle via Bogotá.

BRUCE: I speak for all members of the isolated Amazonian tribe community when I say that the Huitoto people are underrepresented in filmography that deals with anti-transethnic bigotry in San Diego vegan bistros.

LEO & MYRTLE: We are humbled at being called out on our ignorance and will make a better effort to learn about this important conversation.

"We are *all* humbled at being called out on our ignorance. But unfortunately, *we* must call an end to this edition of *Inside the Hactors Studio* since Leo has six flights to catch. As always, I have been your host, Anus Panderson, saying, 'We'll have important conversations soon, Hollywoke. And shame be on us all.'"

5:33 PM

That over there, you ask? She's the in-house feline, Katz. Oh, you mean next to her? That's a boot. For when we need to fire someone, we give them the boot. Yes, they usually do take it with them, hence the stockpile in the backroom, where Katz usually sleeps.

No, nothing else of interest in there, just boots and Katz. I said, "Just boots and Katz"! What are you auditorily defective? Boots and Katz, you fugly tit-baboon! Boots and Katz! Boots and Katz, boots and Katz, boots and Katz!

BOOTS AND CATS AND MYTHS AND FACTS

MYTH: God created the Earth 6,000 years ago.

FACT: Radiocarbon dating along with advances in theology put that number closer to 6,411 years.

MYTH: The Stork delivers babies.

FACT: While modern science has only scratched the surface of the mystery of procreation, the claim that The Stork performs a role in it has been debunked. First, the definite article "The" suggests that one specific stork carries out the deliveries. Given the global birth census as recently as 2023, this hypothesis is untenable: it would require at least 380,000 storks (plural) to account for the daily natal increase worldwide. Second, and more importantly, a stork's bill is ill-suited to hoist a newborn. Within the avian species, the most plausible candidate for this task—though research is yet inconclusive on this—is pelicans.

BOOT: Ь

CAT: =^.^=

MYTH: Mankind's fall from Paradise was the result of Eve tasting the forbidden fruit after being tempted by the snake.

FACT: The unfortunate myth of The Fall has long served as justification for the enduring prejudice against snakes and systemic ophidiophobia of our culture. In truth, it is impossible that the snake could have persuaded Eve of anything, as snakes do not speak English. As any reader of transphobic fantasy novels knows, they speak parseltongue.

MYTH: Witches oil their broomsticks with baby fat to equip them for flight.

FACT: By Coulomb's Law, for the jockey to remain at rest atop the broom, the dry frictional force must be lesser than or equal to the normal force multiplied by the coefficient of friction (for wood: 0.48–0.70). As studies have shown, baby fat yields a lubricated sliding friction coefficient of 0.067, rendering the average witch virtually incapable of remaining saddled during flight. As for the so-called "Quidditch Paradox," a recent theory posits that the weaker gravitational field in and around Hogwarts campus, cast by one Albus Dumbledore, Esq., may explain it.

BOOT: *n.*, A covering for the foot and lower part of the leg.*

CAT: *n.*, A well-known carnivorous quadruped (*Felis domesticus*) which has long been domesticated, being kept to destroy mice, and as a house pet.*

**Oxford English Dictionary*

MYTH: The Earth is flat.

FACT: The conception that the Earth is flat is as old as the Earth itself (approx. 6,411 years), and is likely the result of conflicting interpretations of the word "crust" in the geological term, "the Earth's crust." Understood culinarily, the term suggests that the Earth resembles round and flattened foodstuffs with doughy rims, such as pizza. (The myth that the moon is flat has a similar source, rooted in literal interpretations of how the moon hits your eye according to Dean Martin.)

MYTH: Icarus fell out of the sky because he soared too close to the Sun.

FACT: Icarus's storied fall has been attributed to ill-advisedly lubricating his wings ever since forensic reports confirmed remnants of baby fat in Daedalus's workshop (see Coulomb's Law).

MYTH: Lizard people control the world-government.

FACT: The core temperature of most terrestrial reptiles is 30 °C (86 °F). As such, average thermic conditions of government buildings (discounting airflow) are too hostile for reptiles *or reptile hybrids* to expedite global administrative functions. It is therefore conjectured that the headquarters of these shapeshifting Sionic Elders is a subaquatic habitat (see Mar Tay Greene, Rob Ken Jr., *et al.)*; which, moreover, would not be hospitable to lizard-people, but at best, only to amphibious ungulate-people with blowholes.

MYTH AND CAT: There was an old cat-lady who lived in a shoe.

FACT AND BOOT: She was only twenty-six and it was a galosh.

FACT AND CAT: Did you know that those are not real cats in Cats? They are rotating casts of *humans*, none of whom is named Rum Tum Tugger or Skimbleshanks, who merely dress-up and sing like cats to hoodwink observers for a profit.

MYTH AND BOOT: The iconic German blockbuster *Das Boot* can be perfectly synchronized to Pink Floyd's *Dark Side of the Moon* if you play the album on a loop for four and a half hours.

MYTH AND FACT: If you believe the myth that vaccines cause cognitive impairment, it is already too late for you, so you might as well get vaccinated.

BOOT AND CAT: To illustrate the paradoxical principle of superposition, quantum mechanics uses a thought-experiment in which a steel-toe work boot is simultaneously tied and untied. It is known as "Schrödinger's CAT®."

MYTH AND BOOT AND FACT AND CAT: The name of the cat from the mythical tale *Shrek* is Puss in Boots and that is a fact.

6:06 PM

What kind of an establishment would we be if we had no room for love? I'm not talking about a love room. That is something else entirely, located behind the false wall in my basement and outfitted with shaft clamps of all girths and voltages, exuding that tantalizing scent of ammonia for sterilizing the enema prods.

I see some of you have perked up. Give me your numbers, I'll text you later with the waiver.

So, what does love have to do with it? Little to nothing in my shag shack. But for you sentimentalists out there, it is quaint simple. Harken up.

THE SIMPLEOSIUM

It was one of them Sunday scorchers in lazy Hibillton. Me and the boys—Clyde, Durp, and Squam—moseyed down to the log cabin by babbling Hellas Brook, where we was endeavoring to distill our trough hooch. Cabin didn't feature no cooling system on account of the lack of electric wiring, nor generators to power said absent wiring neither. So to keep 'frigerated, we stripped down to our birthday bests, sporting rags as loincloths to cover the old flesh-bindles. Now, our nephyas—Lil Hank, Lil Bill, Lil Joe, and Lil Joey Hankbill—they kept an eye on the batch and tended to our libational needs with occasional pours of the troughbrew. The nephyas, they too doffed down to nothing but their underdrawers what with the mugsome heat. And whilst me and the boys sipped on them victuals and the youngbloods stood by, all of us milling about in nigh-nude glory, we began to wax philosophic on matters of the heart.

CLYDE: Hey Durp?

DURP: What's that, Clyde?

CLYDE: What do you reckon's the meaning of beauty?

DURP: Hell if I know.

SQUAM: If I may interlocute, what I surmise Clyde here is gesturing at is how'd you go about defining "beauty," such as to consult it in a dictionary book or them interwebs.

DURP: I suppose I'd have to say it's like that famous wisedom: "Beauty's in the eye of the tiger."

SQUAM: *Bee holder*, Durp. It's in the eye of the *bee holder*.

DURP: Ain't that the truth. And as bees house honey in their combs, so the eyes house beauty in their cones.

CLYDE: That's a mighty fine analogy, Durp, mighty fine. But mayn't I prod that rationale with these interrogatives. Say now, do you find Jesus beautiful?

DURP: Be darned if I didn't!

CLYDE: So you would, Durp, so you would. Yet in light of that fine dictum you've just propounded, how'd you'd go about counterarguing them infidels what maintain that Our Lord and Savior—the very portrait of beauty we pure Christians know him to be—is in their estimations a mischievous fraud, assuming they were to adopt your logic? For, way I see it, they might could as well say that beauty is whatsoever happens to occupy *their* eyes. So to them Hebrews, their Moses fella appears most beautiful, while them Mahometans can lawfully celebrate their spelunking Prophet as the very apogee of beauty. Yet meantime, to their unbelieving gaze, our winsome Redeemer might appear as a fugly Porky Pig. Now ain't that be so, Durp?

DURP: The Devil's dingleberries, Clyde! Now why must you go and blaspheme the Lord's good name like that?

SQUAM: Tranquilize yourself there, Durp. It ain't Clyde done besmirched our heavenly bellwether thus. He but *reports* about the heathen lips which allege such cosmetic vulgarities of our fetching Father's son. Clyde's heart is untainted of such affrontitudes. Yet his contention to you is howsoever to define beauty whilst eluding that sacrilege, the which significates that even a heretic's eyes can may dictate what's beautiful merely by pleasing the observer.

CLYDE: Like shiniest pond milk, Squam, you have reflected my intentions with preciselyhood. But tell, have you some resolution to that thorny inquest you done just identified?

SQUAM: Truth be told, way I see it—beauty?—it's that snare of passion, that strikes as a wingèd babe's arrow, through the ribcage, making the ol' whiteytights tumesce with unbridled excitation. It is, should I summon a concrete exemplar, verily what this company of Lil Hank, Lil Bill, Lil Joe, and Lil Joey Hankbill effects in us wizened men by simple virtue of their nubile presence and budding anatomies.

CLYDE: That's some mighty fine poesy there, Squam, might fine. Durp, mightn't you top that exposition?

DURP: If I must venture my own oratory, I challenge that Squam here equivocates betwixt beauty and pleasure. Beauty ain't about the gustatory salacity that Lil Bill here enkindles. Nor ain't it about merely stiffening the wilburys, like Lil Hank here might so provoke. No sir, it's about the *eemotional* connection what can be had with another. Take Lil Joey Hankbill here. Granted, his torso is flush like a seal pup's hide, his buxom thighs soft as velveteen in autumn, being as he is yet unblemished by the wrinkling elapsings of Time. Albeit what corporal amusements he may inspire, however relishable, pale in comparison to the comingling of our profoundest eemotions.

CLYDE: Hootnanny, Durp, I applaud that eloquacious rebuttal. And Squam, so unto you do I tip my proverbial boater for your exquisitory asseverations. But what say *you* of this topic, having remained taciturn heretofore?

ME: If I'm bid speak, let me offer not my own thinklings, but teachings imparted on me by a spritely youth I betimes conjugated by the name of Diotime. Diotime, see, he came upon me last Easter, proclaiming to be the issue of my great auntie's niece's grandson's loins. He told me, so he said, that he would instruct me on the ways of Beauty. So he said, all that is beautiful partakes of Beauty, but Beauty is not selfsame with those things which are beautiful. The way Lil Hank partakes of our nephyas, but Nephyas ain't the same as just Lil Hank or Lil Bill or Lil Joe or Lil Joey Hankbill on account of there's more blooming hoochbearers out there who is also nephyas, yet none by himself nor all together who be identical with Nephyas.

DURP: Doggonit, these musings is making my melon twirl! I say, I behoove another round to help slide those argumentations down. Lil Joe, fertch us hither some more of that sweet sassprilluh!

CLYDE: If I follow your ratiocination, wouldn't it not entail that, if each of these here nephyas is dependent for what defines them upon a higher Nephyas, *that* Nephyas would needs be defined by yet a third one, and so on till infinitude?

SQUAM: Seeing as it should must be defined by that terciary term there, and likewise after it, as Clyde done shown, it could be called a "Third Nephyas" problem.

ME: An astute nomenclature it be indeed, Squam. Howbeit, it just so transpired that young Diotime, whose acquaintance I made not but one Easter ago, is hand-to-heart our *first* nephya, whom no higher term needs define seeing such as he is the original term itself. Now, these nephyas here—Lil Joey Hankbill and the rest of the fledgling lot—we can't excogitate on our proximities to them on account of we don't *know* whose nephyas is whose, what because our wifely consorts not recollecting whom each did sire, whether Squam, Durp, Clyde, myself or any else among our consanguine familials. But see, Diotime, now he is ascertainably fruit of our sororal kin's fertile delta. How do I know? Not by no parlor's flimflam nor medicine man's hoopla, no sir, but by revelation, bestowed by the grace of God, who into our very pigmentation inscribed his covenant with us Fugates.*

SQUAM: You saying this Diotime boy is full-cerulean like us, and not just fourths and eighths like these periwinkle nephyas here?

ME: In very fact and deed, Squam.

DURP: I'll be dagnab diffidy damnated!

CLYDE: Boy howdy, if that ain't Beauty, I don't reckon what is!

ME: It's better than Beauty, Clyde. It's Bleauty.

(*If you don't know the Fugates, look them up. You'll thank me later, doggonit.)

6:55 PM

The phrase "24-hour news cycle" is overused these days, casually tossed by every Bill Blogger and Karen Kommentator like foreskin by a mohel. And like foreskin by a mohel, "The Media" only touches the tip of the issue and dangles it before the gawking gaggle of do-gooders, who are always ready to spread the gospel at the drop of a prepuce.

This hot-off-the-press item honors those feckless fighters at the frontlines of the headlines. Sit back and follow their lede. And you—for the love of Diotime, stop tugging on your prepuce!

NEWSPAPER HEADLIES

SWEEPING SOCIAL MEDIA OVERHAUL BANS USE OF THE TERMS, "SYSTEMIC," "HEGEMONIC," "DEEP STATE," "PATRIARCHAL," "LEFT-WING," "ZIONIST," "INDUSTRIAL COMPLEX," "OTHERING," "COLONIALIST," AND "OFFENSIVE" IN POSTS. USERS BELIEVED OUTRAGED BUT INCAPABLE OF RESPONDING.

The controversial move by tech companies is thought to have infuriated users, as a sharp spike in angry-faced and watermelon emojis suggests. Yet due to the ban, the deeper reflections of the online community on the issue cannot be confirmed. Activists have announced a virtual "kneel-in" to protest the companies, flooding social media platforms from Instagram to TikTok with posts featuring a leg kneeling on a cracked iPad with a caption reading, "The People Will Not Be Programmed."

FRUSTRTION MOUNTS S LETTER ' ' DECOMMISSIONED FROM KEYBORDS CROSS THE GLOBE.

Keybord mnufcturers re slshing costs by cesing production of the beloved letter ' '. When sked for the reson for reclling tht specific chrcter, compnies rgued tht the letter's long edges nd tringulr morphology require specil clligrphers nd extr ink. "It's just smrt business," electronics mgnte, Dvid McNlly insists. The decision hs creted niche for vintge keybords tht still feture the coveted key, which currently sell for 300% mrk-up on the blck mrket.

FROSTY THE SNOWMAN REBRANDED "FROSTY THE SNOWFOLK" AFTER RESEARCH TEAM AT CORNELL DETERMINES THE BELOVED CHILDREN'S CHARACTER LACKS GENITALIA, REPRODUCTIVE CELLS, Y-CHROMOSOMES, AND OTHER IDENTIFIERS DEEMED COMPLICIT IN IMPOSITIONS OF MALE GENDER IDENTITY.

"We traced transgressive and subversive patterns of hermaphroditic projection in various representations of Frosty," says Professor McQuaken, who led the team. "These contradict inherited implicit biases about Frosty's gender, which has been culturally constructed and imposed as male by white men in positions of power, especially within the Yuletide Industrial Complex." McQuaken has been a vocal advocate in the movement to decolonize the phallocratic heritage of the West in favor of a more inclusive view of Frosty, one which does not invalidate the experiences of traditionally disaffected communities of snowpeople and other holiday characters. "Her groundbreaking work has empowered similar projects," fellow academics exclaim. "New research into heteronormative bias against The Tooth Fairy is already underway. Rudolph, The Easter Bunny, even so-called 'Mother' Goose stand to be deconstructed and emancipated from imperialist gender constructs. We are finally having this important conversation."

ENCOURAGING SIGNS OF RECONCILIATION IN A POLARIZED NATION, AS WHITE SUPREMACISTS AND ANTI-FASCISTS MERGE UNDER NEW BANNER.

At a time when "crossing the aisle" is increasingly fraught, common grounds are found among unlikely political bedfellows, which have begun efforts at a bipartisan merger. "We realized we both abhor the Establishment," say advocates, "be it the laws and courts that privilege the banker elites, the taxes that privilege the banker elites, or the intrusive feds that privilege the banker elites. We both oppose the government's involvement in foreign countries to serve the interests of the banker elites. Most of all, we're sick of the banker elites, who rule The System from their Rothschild lairs while the true folk and *Volk* of our country are trampled underfoot." "We still have some differences to iron out," they admit. "But our enemy is the same: the very same that were opposed by the totalitarian regime we faced in WWII and by the totalitarian regime we faced immediately after. The Swasti-Sickle is a step in the direction of unity. It symbolizes our commitment to shared goals and to healing the rift between the silenced ninety-nine percent of the nation."

SATIRICAL HEADLINES MAKE THE ROUNDS IN ROGUE PUBLICATION, CONFUSING AND ANGERING READERS.

"They weren't published by *The Onion* or *The Beaverton*," said one affected reader. "I couldn't figure out where the author was on the political spectrum. How can I be sure whether I'm supposed to agree?" A second reader preached that the publication "unseats the conviction that the opinions 'we identify with' are so sacrosanct and precious. If our opinions can't handle a joke, how are we supposed to overcome actual adversity?" "That second reader is a bigoted enabler," a third reader remarked. "Offensive discourse is implicit manslaughter, mean jokes are ouchie, and our most vulnerable communities need to be guarded against them. That kind of writing needs to be put on a list banning publications that are opposed to correct equity, morals, and truths. If only there were such a list."

CATHOLIC CHURCH REJOICES AS ITS *INDEX OF FORBIDDEN BOOKS* MAKES A COMEBACK.

7:27 PM

The last time I got laid, and I'm talking proper spit roasted, happened to be during an actual roast. It proved a bitching combination, so we decided to make it a weekly ritual; like the Brits on Sundays, except without the sexual repression or dental tragedies.

The result was redundant: I ate pork while getting porked and gained pounds while being pounded. If I'd been pawning my poon to the Brits, I could have added pounds to pounds and given the phrase "pound of flesh" a whole new meaning.

"What if you had been in France? I'm glad I asked."

I'm glad you asked too, Bert. Right this way, mes chéris.

ZE TEMPTATIONS OF COOKING
BY MARQUIS DE SADE

Bienvenue mon amie to ze delighting ecstasies of hot cuisine. For zis dish, you will need a leather apròn with open backend, one sharp razor, a baster for basting, a whip for whipping, and a long thermometer for pricking ze meat, in and out, in and out. A safe word is encouraged but not required.

Dish: Mother Daughter Ménage (Chicken and Eggs Royale)

Preparation time: 45 minutes or until climax

Ingredients:

2 chicken breasts, perky and firm
2 impressively large eggs
½ cup of thick, silky cream
Zome breadcrumbs
Rosemary for seasoning
Rosemarie for intimacy
Zalt and pepper to taste
1 banana hammock
Optional: nipple clamps for ze breasts

Instructions:

Preheat oven to steamy.

First phase is ze eggs. Grip eggs and gently shuffle zem in your palm. If eggs are not shuffling smoothly, apply warm butter for lubrication. Once ze eggs are suitably fondled, pump your fist and swiftly crush zem to bits. Permit ze runny interiors to ooze into a large bowl. Detect any remaining shells and situate in a separate dish. (Do not discard! Ze shells may now be used for extra stimulation during cooking. Chef recommends inserting bits of shell under ze fingernails for spontaneous stabs of delicate torture.)

Now, to whip ze eggs. Retrieve your whip of choice—Chef Sade prefers *le chat à neuf queues*: ze "cat of nine tails"—and increase whipping motion gradually, but sensually. Eggs should obtain a frothy consistency, like bubbles in jacuzzi of love.

Next, handle ze breasts. Violently massage breasts to release moisture and juices. Once breasts are tender and ready, use ze razor to cut off excess flesh. Test sharpness of razor on ze cartilage part of your nose, and prepare for exquisite pain. If razor slices through, it is suitable for employing on ze breasts. Set aside piece of nose for garnish.

Submerge ze tender breasts into egg foam and glide across bowl, like a summer swim in champagne. Zis technique is called ze mother-daughter breaststroke. Ze breasts should now be coated in a shiny membrane, like *mademoiselles* tanning *sur la plage.*

Roll ze breasts in zome breadcrumbs. Ze grainy exterior of ze breasts is now suitable for grating your skin like a sheet of sandpaper. Part ze backend of apròn and scrape a buttock of your choosing, rubbing vigorously. Apply zalt and pepper on ze open wound. Zis effect will rouse pain receptors in pelvic region.

With ze pelvic region adequately roused, it is time for engaging banana hammock. Select a long, throbbing *banane.* If zis is your first time engaging a banana hammock, it is recommended using honey to douse *la banane.* Flap open backend of apròn. Calculating aim, skillfully thrust *banane* into hammock. *Voilà!* Your banana hammock is ready.

While tantric shock of banana probe persists, introduce breasts into steamy oven and heat a saucepan over high. To test heat of ze pan, remove it after *cinq minutes* and press it to your open backend, where *la banane* is currently impaled. If pan is sufficiently heated, you will undergo a sophisticated cascade of torment. Once ready, pour ze thick, silky cream into pan. When cream is bubbling, employ baster to pump a small amount. Point baster into eyes and release smoldering cream into retina for agonizing optic delight.

Add rosemary to ze hot cream. Zen, ask Rosemarie to remove ze banana hammock in one swift extraction. Take moment to relish ze blissful cruelty. If employing nipple clamps, slash Rosemarie's blouse with ze razor to expose her chest and proceed to attach ze clamps to her bodacious *mamelles.* While she howls with erotic anguish, retrieve ze thermometer and plunge it into ze open wound on your buttock, in and out, in and out, to maximize titillation.

By zis moment, ze chicken should be adequate for consumption. Open ze steamy oven and place your bare hands directly on ze piping hot tray. Proceed to bask in paroxysms of scorching glory on your extremities. Examine whether ze chicken is cooked through by clasping one breast in each seared palm of your hand and, with determined force, thrust one, zen another, at Rosemarie's *visage.* Slap her twice on each cheek with ze breasts; zen, repeat procedure on her lower cheeks. If slaps emit a low pitch, *le poulet* is ready. You may now dispatch Rosemarie back to ze *boudoir.*

Enfin, it is time for plating. Situate breasts on ze plate and drizzle cream on top. Do not forget slice of nose to garnish! Zen, carefully peel *la banane.* Discard peel on ze floor and introduce ze whole *banane* into your throat, proceeding to swallow. While gagging on *la banane,* blindly stagger in your proximate orbit. If performed correctly, you shall slip on ze peel and be rewarded with sweet intoxication of unexpected injury.

Hobble à la table with your fresh meal and strap a cloth bib to neck, tightening until achieving pleasant suffocation. You are now ready to dive into ze saucy delicacy of Mother Daughter Ménage!

Bon appétit!

** If you enjoyed ze excruciating pleasure of zis dish as much as *moi,* why not attempt another recipe from my book, *120 Glaze of Sodom?* **

7:59 PM

To those of you who made it to the end of the tour, I salute you. To those who did not, I hope you get royally cornholed by The Mighty Thunder Rod.

Don't forget to incorporate your commentation and make your voices herd by leaving a review. Or don't. Frankly, I don't give a gerbil's teat whether you express your ownmost feelings to the online community. Tell me you don't like me to my face, shit-petard, and afterwards we can enjoy a tipple of mommy's happy juice.

A fitting quote is apocryphally attributed to Voltaire, that foppish Frenchman: "I disapprove of what you say, but I will defend to the death your right to say it." But I *won't defend to the death your right to post it, subtweet it, bump it, or troll it, because what I disapprove of is not what you say but what your identity says you ought to say.*

Next time you are at the hardware store, purchase a sledgehammer, lug it home, and in one fell swoop visit it upon the buzzbot of your group identity. You may be amazed at what you find beneath the wreckage. It is not things people say, but a person with something to *say.*

One last thing—by which I don't mean one last Norse tradition of collective decision-making. Be dolls and spread the word about our satire shop, the old-fashioned way. To make it easy for you, here's a brochure. Literally here. In your hands.

I leave you with this, which is what I tell my weekend paramours. You're good for coming, you're great for staying, and you're even greater for knowing when to leave.

Time to be the greater weekend paramour. We did our fucking around. Now kindly do your fucking off.

SORRY, WE'RE CLOSED

PRAISE FOR *BERTRAM'S EMPORIUM OF THINGS PEOPLE SAY*

Couldn't put this book down! (I tried everything from lethal injections to firing squads.)
—The Bite-Sized Bulletin

This rustic's compendium rivals the very devil's sable scripts. Vex and vim vulgarize its every syllable, the which the author's quill disgorges onto the page like a brothelman's spouting javelin. Malcontent vituperations suffuse the whole, and each chronicle in't sores the peruser's eye like an incarnadine boil fit for lancing. To none do I this bilious tome commend, and would rather its epitaph engrave upon Time's gaping catacomb than undersign its warrant of praise. 'Tis an o'erfangled composition: slender in substance, penurious in offering, fallow in opinion, and barren in craft. And as the work, so its maker be all of these, yet the more blameful for foisting this festerfilled folio on the folk and file of this fair globe. Fie!
—Bard's Bazaar

This book is *so* problematic. My daughterboy, Onyx, heard that someone read a post about this book by trans-ethnic hero, Bruce Lee Jender, who bravely called out how deeply post-traumatic it is to victims of non-privilege. I totes bump that, and strongly petition for the *white male* who wrote it to apologize for his ignorance and make a better effort to learn about this important conversation. BTW, Onyx has already drafted the petition using a strictly diverse, equitable, and inclusive color pallet. Hashtag proudmommydaddy!

—Yum Mum Monthlies

We here at Gringos have an upbeat saying that dates to our agency's infancy, back when we were a humble charter airline. "If it's broken, don't fix it." Those words of wisdom apply to this collection of gags; or should we say, this *gagging* collection? We actually had the opportunity to visit this "Emporium," and believe you we, it is *not* worth the paper on which the airfare there was printed. As it turns out, we found no such Emporium at all, even with the aid of our trusty farmer's almanac. If the hoax of luring innocent globetrotters to an imaginary destination weren't bad enough, our crew was led, of all places, to the poutine-touting tundra of Upper America, where the supposed creator of that supposed Emporium supposedly resides. Someone give me an "eh" for eh-hole!

—Gringos Travel Guide

With ze exception of one saucy *historiette,* zis sexless saga is more *dépravé* than a young libertine's nocturnal emissions, only sans ze libidinous *recherché.* If, like *moi,* you crave ze gastronomique delicacies of untrammelled bestiality, zis collection is destined to abandon you with ze turquoise testicles of unrequited passion. It is not ze chef's recommendation to elect zis dish for your next gustatory philanderie. *Tas de merde!*

—Penthouse Dungeon

I don't always write reviews, but when I do, it's for women's lingerie. I don't always test the lingerie myself, but when I do, I dab on some rouge and bundle my flesh-bindle under my grundle. Until then, I don't always feel like the most interesting man in the world, but when I do, I feel like the most fabulous also. I don't always describe things as fabulous, but when I do, I rate them *dos equis*—out of which this publication deserves a *cero*.

—The Memeington Post

As my moist, glistening fingers, still temperate from the velveteen delta they had just massagingly caressed, thumbed through a fascimilous copy of this book, the lingering ecstasy of my autoerotic care-session fadingly decayed, leaving me gelidly shivering; like that last time that Christian's pulsating pleasure-pole brushed my ungarmented thigh as if to whisper, "Goodbye, forever." My ravenous clitoral voracity, spurned by his churlish departure, became even more withdrawn, recoiling like Christian's porcelain tusk in cold bathwater, after reading this collection of garishly overcomposed unrisible smut.

—E. L. James for *Queef Quarterly*

What we done git ourselves here is an endeavor by another individual of the Hebrew persuasion to sacrilege the True Word of our burly Redeemer. It is some mighty unfine prose, mighty unfine, the which accurses these pages and beheckles the familial proximities of the flesh that are the backbone of the backwoods of this spangled republic. This abominable volume should musts be kept from genuwine patriots, lest its liberal snowflakery pollutes the minds of our great nation's fetching red, white, and blue nephyas.

—The Kentucky Kronikle

The author wrote farcical reviews of his own book voiced by its characters as a self-deprecating ironic gag, which the readers would immediately realize was ironic, thus undoing the irony. And yet, that irony would itself be undone by the further ironic gesture of making explicit reference to the double irony of the gag within another farcical review that was itself self-referentially ironic. Indeed, the self-referentially ironic voice of that ironic farcical review was itself a reference to a character that featured in the book whose superpower was that of meta-reference, meaning that the meta-reference of the ironic farcical review ironically meta-referenced a meta-referential character. And given that the author was clearly commenting on the meta-commentary of the meta-commenting character's commentary, it redoubled the quadruple irony, making it an 8-iron, which is a short club. And this is a collection of shorts that deserves to get clubbed.

—David Foster Wallace for *Meta Mag* for "Praise for *Bertram's Emporium of Things People Say*" for *Bertram's Emporium of Things People Say.*

Neoproblematic. Macroaggressive. Anti-TAMPPoNMaP. These are the semiotic referents that our herstorical deconstruction of this publication reveal. As the sacrificial lamb for the sins of Caucasian hegemony, I am uniquely affected by this act of Empire that implicitly disenfranchises the Truth of my important conversation. It is imperative—nay, imperative—to boycott both the disablism, racism, homophobism, and fascism of this manpressive manifesto. Not since J. K. Rowling have members of the traditionally dismembered community been genocided by such metatextual violence. Two antiphallic thumbs down.

☹☹☹☹☹

—The Hollywoke Culture Review

I kind of liked it, squire. Nudge, nudge, wink, wink.

—Ariel, former employee of Bertram's Boutique of Thoughts People Had.

ACKNOWLEDGEMENTS

This is my first published book. Had it not been for the support of a few very important people, it would have joined the proverbial wastebin in which my other two or three books languish unpublished, and possibly unpublishable. That this attempt succeeded was not only a function of steadily improving my writing ever since I developed a regimented discipline over a decade ago, nor just a consequence of taking a hard humorist turn. Beyond all else, it owes to those who appreciated something unique in my writing, encouraged me to continue doing it, and most importantly, enjoyed reading it.

To my friends, family, and the precious few strangers who by cosmic luck stumbled upon my work in the vast hinterland of digital content: thank you for reading my short pieces when I first started publishing them on Medium. The fact that someone other than myself and the drill sergeant inside my head, someone *out there*, was reading them, getting them, and getting something out of them, meant the world to me. The occasional share, the privately conveyed words of praise, the affirmations that laughter was taking place in the void and that my writing was eliciting it—these small gestures resounded like thunderclaps. You let me know that I was doing something right, perhaps even of importance, and lit a fire under my ass to keep me at it. You all have a hand in the writing of this book.

Thanks to the Medium page, "Down in the Dingle," where I first started publicly sharing my short pieces, many of which have made it into this collection. Without that platform to share my work and the initial public validation that it was striking a chord, I may not have continued my foray into humorist writing and satirical social commentary.

My most immense debt of gratitude is owed to the fearless team at Vine Leaves Press for putting an end to the tsunamic stream of rejection letters in my inbox. The doubletake when I first saw their reply was like noticing a glitch in The Matrix. My evolution from writer to author took place between the lines, "We would very much like to read more ..." and "We would love to publish this" a few exchanges later, when with unflinching conviction they committed to invest time, money, resources, and staff to the publication of my work based solely on a strong belief in its merit and potential. My deepest thanks to Jessica Bell for seeing this value in my work; to Alexis Paige for her sharp editorial eye, with which she expertly guided me towards making the manuscript publication-worthy; to Amie McCracken for logistically masterminding the publication process; and to Melissa Slayton for spearheading the developmental edit of my book and prompting the astute finishing touches.

In lieu of a partner to thank last on the list, as is customary in these acknowledgments' sections, I thank my cat, Oliver, who provided much needed company during the isolation of quarantine and the solitary hours, days, weeks, and months spent writing this book, and writing generally since. For this, he has been, and continues to be, rewarded with decadent meals of former marine life.

VINE LEAVES PRESS

Enjoyed this book?
Go to *vineleavespress.com* to find more.
Subscribe to our newsletter:

* 9 7 8 3 9 8 8 3 2 0 9 1 9 *
ND - #0116 - 011124 - C0 - 229/152/12 - PB - 9783988320919 - Matt Lamination